D0969540

REVIEW

"Well, Walt Williams strikes again, and I enjoyed the adventure ... Keep up the good work!"

—Lee Dresser, The Krazy Kats, Author of *Was There A Band Here Tonight?*

"Old folks with Viagra-free staying power. Think Matlock on steroids. Thornhill may have created a new genre ... Walt and the gang return for another round of snappy one-liners and fast-paced vignettes that will leave readers begging for the next installment and criminals begging him to retire again ...

Thornhill doesn't get bogged down in heavy prose or tedious dialogue. Readers from eighteen to ninety-eight will giggle openly at the lighthearted puns and delightful tongue-in-cheek wordplay. An ageless story told with a genuine style."

—Michael Clutton, Author of *Juice Revolution*

"Bob's first book caught me off guard so many times. His idioms and phrases are priceless. When I wasn't expecting it, I would be hit with something that made me laugh so hard I cried!

With the second book, I was already hooked on the characters. They are each endearing in their own way, and I love [Walt's] way of finding the good in people whom most would just judge as they would a book cover. [Bob's] writing grabs your interest from the beginning and will leave you wanting the stories to just continue on."

—Vicky Mitzner

"We were delighted to read Lady Justice and the Lost Tapes! This book is laugh-out-loud funny. We didn't want to put it down as we turned each page, anxious to see what would come next."

—Lee and Marilyn Dobbins

"Walt Williams and his trusty band of senior citizen peacekeepers are once again making Kansas City a safer place in *Lady Justice and the Lost Tapes*! From solving a mafia-engineered land scheme to celebrating the music of the King (Elvis), this second installment of Bob Thornhill's Lady Justice Series is a must-read for anyone who enjoys lighthearted detective stories. Walt's undercover misadventures are a riot. I laughed all the way through. If you're looking for a book to tickle your funny bone, this is it!"

—Mary Carmean, Office Operations Administrator, RE/MAX Heartland

LADY JUSTICE

AND THE

LOST TAPES

A WALT WILLIAMS
MYSTERY/COMEDY NOVEL

ROBERT THORNHILL

3

Lady Justice and the Lost Tapes

Volume #2

Second Edition

Copyright August, 2014 by Robert Thornhill

First Edition

Copyright December, 2010 by Robert Thornhill

All rights reserved.

No part of this publication may be reproduced, stored in a retrieval system or transmitted in any way, by any means, electronic, mechanical, photocopy, recording or otherwise without prior permission of the author except as provided by USA copyright law.

This novel is a work of fiction. Names, incidents and entities included in the story are products of the author's imagination. Any resemblance to actual persons, events and entities is entirely coincidental.

Published in the United States of America

    1. Fiction, Humorous
    2. Fiction, Mystery & Detective, General

DEDICATION

To my good friend, Lee Dresser
The Krazy Kats

May 22, 1941 – April 24, 2014

A rocker 'til the very end!

PROLOGUE

Salvatore Lorenzo took a long drag of his Cuban cigar, exhaled and watched as the smoke rose to the ceiling.

"So Councilman, how much money are we talking about?"

Already apprehensive, sitting across from the godfather of the Kansas City mob, Manny Delano cleared his throat and collected his thoughts.

"Millions, Mr. Lorenzo; Urban renewal brings in millions! Examples are Quality Hill, the Power & Light District, the Glover Plan, just to name a few. Once the City Council approves a project, State, Federal and local money starts pouring in to buy up the property in the target area. Tear-downs and board-ups that weren't worth spit are suddenly going for ten times their market value."

Lorenzo flipped an ash onto the floor. "And you're sure you have enough votes to get this thing through the City Council?"

Delano drew a deep breath. "Yes, Sir. I believe I do. No--- I'm certain that I do."

"You'd better be," Lorenzo replied. "If I decide to divert funds from our other projects and this thing goes south --- well, your district will be looking for someone to fill the sudden vacancy in your council seat. Do you get my drift?"

"Yes, I understand."

"Good. Now tell me about this target area."

Delano spread a map across the table. "The boundaries are the freeway on the west side, Paseo on the east, Independence Avenue on the north and Truman Road on the south."

Lorenzo studied the map. "So what's there now?"

Delano turned to Michael and Constance Lorenzo who has been listening intently to the councilman's presentation. "I'll let Connie speak to that question. Riverfront Realty has served that area for years and Connie knows every inch of it."

Connie tapped her finger on the map. "Definitely a blighted area. Hookers and drug dealers on every corner. The majority of the single family homes are rentals but there are a few older, long term owners that still keep their property up hoping things will turn around.

"The businesses are what you'd expect, liquor stores, porn shops, bars and night clubs and convenience stores."

Lorenzo pondered a moment. "So what are our chances of acquiring the majority of these properties discreetly before the City Council announces the Urban Renewal Project to the public?"

"Connie and I can handle the acquisition of the single family homes, Uncle Sal," Michael Lorenzo replied. "The businesses are another story. Some of them have been operating for decades. They may be reluctant to sell."

"I think we can persuade obstinate owners to consider a reasonable offer." He turned to his long-time partner. "What do you think, Emile?"

Emile Mancuso smiled. "Joey Piccolo can be very persuasive. I don't think we'll have a problem there. But I do have another concern. We will be diverting funds from our drug and protection operations into Eastside Properties, Inc. to buy up the parcels. If the cops go sniffing around, the whole thing could blow up on us. We need someone in the KCPD to keep tabs on police operations in the area. Any ideas?"

"Not to worry, Emile," Lorenzo replied. "I just happen to know a captain that has had a run of bad luck at the Riverboat Casino. He's in debt to us so deep he'll never see the light of day on his salary. He'll play ball."

"Then it sounds like everything is in place," Mancuso said, looking around the room. "Michael, you and Connie start working on those single family homes. I'll have Joey get the hookers and druggies out of the neighborhood and Sal, you get us that cop. Let's do this!"

CHAPTER 1

As I drove to the precinct station, I suddenly noticed that Mother Nature was starting her fall makeover.

There had been a bite in the air, and as I drove down the tree-lined boulevards of Kansas City, I saw the leaves starting to take on the browns, reds, and bright yellows of fall.

Where had the summer gone?

Just a few short months ago, I was bored to death, realizing that retirement wasn't all it was cracked up to be. Then, one morning, I witnessed the mugging of an elderly lady and I knew that Lady Justice had a job for me to do.

It wasn't easy getting into the police department at the ripe old age of sixty-five, but with the help of my old high school chum, Captain Short, I not only became a full-fledged officer, I was also put in charge of a new program for senior recruits, The City Retiree Action Patrol.

Before my involvement in the police department and the C.R.A.P. program, time seemed to drag on, but the last few months had flown by. Having a purpose in life and living your dream gives you a new lease on life, no matter what your age.

I parked, and as I entered the building, I met Captain Harrington and Lincoln Murdock.

To say that I was not one of their favorite people would be a gross understatement.

Captain Harrington had fought against me becoming an officer and the C.R.A.P. program from the beginning. It didn't help that I had shot him with a Benford #5 taser in front of the other captains.

Murdock was just a jerk. He gave me grief whenever he could, but Ox, my partner, and Vince, my first recruit in the new program, had convinced him to back off.

Doing my best to be cordial, I said, "Good morning," and went out of my way to steer clear of their path.

Just as we passed, Murdock swerved and collided with me, knocking me into the wall.

"Hey, old timer. You better get yourself some glasses so you can see where you're going." He and Harrington went off chuckling to themselves.

What a great way to start the day.

Then I remembered something the professor, one of the tenants in my apartment building, told me. "Eat a live toad in the morning and nothing worse will happen to you the rest of the day."

I've just had my toad, I thought. *The rest of the day will be a breeze.*

Our assignment for the day was to serve bench warrants from the Sixteenth Circuit Court.

A bench warrant is issued by a judge most typically when a perp fails to appear for his court date or comply with a court order. Police have the authority to pick up the subject and bring them before the court.

Our perp was Marvin "Blackie" Mercer. He allegedly ran a chop shop on Prospect Avenue and was arrested for possession of a stolen vehicle. He had missed his court date.

We pulled into the parking lot of Mercer's garage. The big bay door was open, and we saw a stocky man in a leather apron with a welding torch.

He was as big as Ox and wore a red bandana around his head. A heavy chain ran from his belt to a set of keys hanging out of his pocket.

Typical biker.

A woman was standing behind him with a beer in her hands and a sneer on her lips.

"Marvin Mercer?" Ox said as we approached.

"Don't call me Marvin! The name's Blackie. Whadda you want?"

"Well, Blackie, we have a warrant for your arrest. You missed your court date."

"And you two punk cops think you're gonna take me in?"

He reached for a can of aerosol spray paint, held it in front of the flaming torch, and pushed the button.

The red spray from the can ignited as it passed through the torch and sent a flaming red stream in our direction.

Homemade flamethrower!

I remembered from high school, some of the guys would get together after a meal of refried beans. They would take a cigarette lighter and ignite one another's farts.

That was fun. This, not so much.

Ox and I stumbled backwards, away from the searing flames, tripped on a power cord, and fell in a heap.

Mercer dropped the torch and headed for the door. "Get your butt in gear, Wanda. Let's get out of here."

They both ran out the door, and as we were untangling ourselves, we heard the unmistakable rumble of a Harley.

We got to the door just in time to see Marvin take off with Wanda behind him holding on for dear life.

Marvin gunned it and did a wheelie. Wanda slipped off the back and landed on her butt. As he drove away, we saw the back of his t-shirt, which read, "If you can read this, the bitch fell off."

Irony!

We jumped in our black and white, and with sirens blaring and lights flashing, we took off after Marvin.

Our old Crown Vic had seen better days. We knew there was no way we were going to catch Marvin on his Harley.

We called dispatch and told them we were in pursuit of a fleeing felon, going south on Prospect. All units in the area were alerted. They would converge on the area and try to cut him off.

We could see Mercer gaining ground on us. But in the distance we saw the flashing lights of another cruiser that had blocked the intersection.

Mercer slowed down and hung a left on Thirty-fifth Street. We were catching up. As he picked up speed, another black and white appeared from a side street, cutting him off.

At the last minute, he swerved and plowed into the open doorway of a huge garage. The sign above the door said, "Earl Shine Automotive. We'll Paint Any Car For $99." We pulled up outside the bay door and looked inside.

Mercer had crashed into an Earl Shine paint booth that was in the process of painting a Yugo bright red.

Blackie wasn't black anymore!

I remembered the professor saying, "Man who drive like hell bound to get there."

Lady Justice loves her irony.

CHAPTER 2

I was feeling pretty good as I drove home from the station. There's a real satisfaction in bringing the bad guys to justice.

I parked, and as I walked up the sidewalk, I met Willie. "Evenin, Mr. Walt."

Willie took care of the maintenance on my huge portfolio of apartments before I retired and sold the whole kit and caboodle. He sort of retired with me, and now he lives in the basement studio of my Armour building and looks after things here and at my only other building, the Three Trails Hotel.

"Good evening to you, Willie. What's up?"

"I got a favor to axe you, Mr. Walt. You member my fren Maxine what works de corner at Independence and Prospect? Well, she call me and said dat Doris, who works at Independence and Troost, ain't been seen fo two days. She an' de other girls is real worried about her."

"Has anyone made a missing persons report to the police?"

"Come on, Mr. Walt. You know betta dan dat. Doris ain't got no family, and de other girls don't want no part of de po-lice. And besides, who's gonna care? She jus another ole black ho to de cops."

"I suppose you're right. Let's take a drive over to Independence Avenue and see what's going on."

We drove east on Armour and north on Prospect to Independence Avenue. Sure enough, there on the corner was Maxine dressed in six-inch heels, black spandex leotards, and a gold v-necked sweater that showed lots of cleavage.

"That girl's a real pro." Willie beamed.

I'll take his word for it.

We pulled to the curb, and Willie called for Maxine to get in.

"Maxine, this is my friend Walt I was telling you about. He's okay. He's gonna hep us find Doris."

"Hi, Maxine. When did you last see Doris?"

"It was two days ago. We bof went to work 'bout eight o'clock. I ain't seen her since."

"Is it possible she hooked up with someone who wanted an, uh, extended visit?"

"Nope. We always tells each other if we got an all-nighter so's the other girls don't get worried. We look out after each other."

"Where did Doris live? Has anyone checked her apartment?"

"She live over on Eighth Street, jus' a few blocks from her corner. I got a key, but I was scared to go der by mysef."

"You're not alone now," I said. "Let's go take a look."

As we drove along Independence Avenue, I noticed that as we got closer to Troost there were more abandoned board-ups and homes for sale.

"What's going on around here?" I asked. "Things look awfully quiet and deserted."

"Yeah, somethin's going on for sure lately. All the action seems to be movin' east in my direction. Don't know why."

We pulled up in front of Doris's building and went to her apartment. I took the key from Maxine and slipped it in the lock. I pushed the door open and called Doris's name.

No answer.

We stepped in the door, and I flipped the light switch on.

I saw a blur of yellow out of the corner of my eye and a loud mew and a "Holy shit!" from Willie as a big, furry ball latched onto his chest.

As Willie was screaming and dancing around trying to separate himself from his attacker, Maxine said, "For gosh sake, Willie. It's just Punkin', Doris's cat. He's probably lonesome."

"Damn!" Willie said. "Dat's de firs' time I been skeered by a pussy!"

We looked around the apartment, and it was apparent that no one had been there in several days. The cat's food and water bowl were empty, and his litter box was full.

I saw a photograph in a frame on an end table and did a double take. There was the photo of a woman that I assumed was Doris and a younger man—Willie!

Willie saw me staring at the photo. "Yeah, dat's me. Doris an' me had a thing once."

"Must have been pretty special," I said. "Having your photo here after all these years."

"I always treats my ladies right. Don't I, Maxine?"

"Sho do, Willie. She always had a sof' spot in her heart fo' you. You know, Mr. Walt, people drive

16

down de street and all de see is ole street ho's, but we people too, and we got feelin's jus' like everyone else."

And she was right.

"Has Doris mentioned anything unusual happening in the last few weeks?"

"Well, now that you mention it, she tole me she had a visit from Joey Piccolo. He works for de Italian mob guys. He tole her she betta move her black ass to another corner or she be sorry. An' she tole him dat she been workin' dat corner fo' ten years an she ain't about to move now."

"Did the mob want to take over the corner for themselves?" I asked.

"No, don't tink so. De been concentraten' on de northeast area. Haven't been given any of us a hassle up till now."

We put out some food and water for Pumpkin, cleaned his litter box, and locked up.

We drove back to Independence and Prospect, and as I was letting Maxine out of the car, a car pulled up in front of me and one behind me. Two guys got out of each car and approached my driver's door.

"Please step of the car, sir," he ordered. "You too, punk," he said to Willie.

"Who you calling punk?" Willie bellowed.

Maxine was already in cuffs and leaning against the car.

"Sir, you're under arrest for solicitation. You have the right to remain silent—"

17

"No, wait a minute," I shouted. "My name's Walter Williams. I'm a cop!"

"Yeah," the officer replied. "And I'm Simon Cowell. We saw you in the car with this pimp and saw you pick up his girl, and we followed you to her apartment. Hope you enjoyed yourself, buddy."

"I ain't no pimp!" Willie shouted.

"Well, you sure ain't Sammy Davis," he snickered. "Now all of you get your hands behind your backs." He cuffed us and threw us in the unmarked car.

Officer Friendly was herding us to the booking desk when we met Captain Short in the hall.

"Good God, Walt! What are you doing in cuffs? Officer Barrett, release this man immediately. He's one of us."

"Well then, what was he doing with this hooker and her pimp?" he asked.

"I keep tellin' you I ain't no pimp!" Willie shouted.

"Okay," Shorty said, "let's take this to a conference room and sort things out."

Within an hour, we had shared our story, filed a missing persons report on Doris, and were transported back to my car by Officer Friendly.

"I hope there's no hard feelings," he said as he let us out of the car.

"Nope, you were just doing your job," I replied.

But as he drove away, Willie flagged him a bird and shouted, "An' I ain't no pimp!"

We were driving down Troost, and I saw a huge, old abandoned warehouse with a new sign in bright

18

red letters that read "The House From Hell." I slowed down for a better look and saw that it was one of those places that open up just for the Halloween season.

There are probably a half dozen of these creepy old buildings around town that are turned into haunted houses, and people pay five bucks a head to walk through and get the crap scared out of them.

Young college kids are hired to dress as goons, goblins, ghosts, and other creepy stuff to scare the bejeezus out of the paying customers.

"Willie, do you think any of this could be drug related?"

"Don't got no idea. I know Doris didn' do drugs. An' you know I nevah had nothin' to to with no drugs. Dey affect yo performance, you know. An' I got a reputation to protect. But I know somebody who might know somethin'."

"And who would that be?"

"Louie de Lip. Head down to Prospect an' St. John. He's usually der."

We pulled up to St. John, and Willie said, "Der he is. On de corner. You keep quiet an' let me talk to him first so he don't run."

I let Willie out of the car, and he went up to Louie. They did that goofy handshake, arm pump, shoulder bump thing that cool guys do. I never could figure it out.

In a minute, Louie came over to the car and got in the backseat.

I saw why he was called Louie the Lip. He made Mick Jagger look like an amateur.

"I'm only talking to you 'cause Willie says you're okay. Now what do you want to know?"

"I understand that you have some knowledge of, uh, pharmaceuticals. Please understand. I'm not Narcotics. I'm not here to hassle you. We're just trying to find out what happened to Doris. It looks like something funny is going on in the Independence and Troost area."

"You got that right. Everything has been weird for a while. The Italian mob used to run things, but then the Russian mob moved in. They owned the streets for a while; then you guys busted them and the Italians moved back in again. Just like old times.

"I'm just a little guy. The mob never paid any attention to me until about a month ago. Then one day I got a visit from Joey Piccolo. He says to me that if I want to stay healthy I need to move my operation away from Independence and Troost. 'To where?' I ask him, and he says anywhere but there. So here I am, and I haven't heard a word from them since."

"Any idea why they wanted you to move?"

"Not a clue. I thought maybe they wanted an exclusive on that area, but nothing's been going down there since I left."

"Thanks for your help, Louie."

"No problem."

But as he stepped out of the car, two unmarked cars moved in front and back of us.

"Okay. Hands in the air where I can see them."

Officer Friendly moved up to the window with gun drawn. "Not you again."

"Don't you vice guys have anything to do but bust honest citizens?" I said with a grin. "My friends and I were just doing some follow-up on the conversation we had with Captain Short."

He gave Louie the Lip a skeptical glance, holstered his gun, and walked away muttering, "Why can't these old farts just go somewhere and play bingo?"

As he drove away, Willie reminded him, "I ain't no pimp."

I hope we got that settled.

I wanted to get another look at the neighborhood, so I suggested that we might come back tomorrow.

Maybe we could even walk through The House From Hell.

I called my sweetie, Maggie, and asked if she would like to go to hell with me.

"Might as well," she said. "You've already taken me to Mel's Diner."

Funny girl.

I picked Maggie up after work the next day and swung by my apartment to change clothes and get Willie.

"Guess what, Mr. Walt?" Willie said. "I told Mary we were going to the haunted house, and she wants to come too."

Swell!

Mary is the house mother of the Three Trails Hotel that I own. I'll admit it --- it's a flop house. Twenty sleeping rooms share four hall baths. My tenants are mostly old retired guys on Social Security or guys working the day labor pool. They're a crusty bunch and somebody has to be on site to keep order. That person is Mary. She's a young seventy-something, but rules the place with an iron hand.

I picked up Mary at the Three Trails, and we headed off to get the poop scared out of us.

As we drove along, I noticed little kids in costume with parents in tow, going door to door begging for candy. It reminded me of my own youthful Halloweens.

I grew up in Harrisonville, a small town about an hour south of Kansas City.

Trick or treating was certainly different in 1950 than it is today. Modern parents wouldn't dream of letting their kids loose with all the perverts and weirdoes out there putting drugs and razor blades in the candy.

For us, Halloween was a game that if played masterfully would yield a huge shopping bag overflowing with sweet delights.

Halloween, if done correctly, was pretty much a weeklong event. We would dress up and go out in pairs so that we could cover as much ground as possible. We kept track of the loot we received at each house. The ones giving sticks of gum, individually wrapped hard candy, or horror of horrors, an apple, were blackballed. But the ones giving full-sized candy bars were put on the list.

We would meet the next day and exchange addresses with other pairs of our friends so that we could hit one another's hot spots with the big candy bars.

Quite a system.

We also carried the trick essentials in case we ran into an old grouch or grump. The two stock items were Ivory soap and a roll of toilet paper. If we ran into a "get off my porch," the offender would find the windows of his car covered with Ivory the next morning.

No harm really. After all, it washes right off.

If someone were particularly offensive, he would find his trees and shrubs draped with super-soft toilet tissue the next morning.

It's so much simpler just to give a kid a candy bar. I never did it, but some of the rougher kids found it amusing to tip over outhouses on Halloween.

As I thought about the changes in sixty years, I thought about that old bar of Ivory. Its claim to fame, other than being good for soaping car windows, was that it was 99 and 44/100 pure and 'It Floats.'

Not anymore.

They've added stuff that makes it not so pure, and now it sinks just like all the rest.

Am I the only one who wonders if this is really progress?

As we drove through the neighborhood around the haunted house, I pointed out all the board-ups and houses for sale.

"I need you to do me a favor," I said to Maggie. "You still have access to the Multiple Listing Service. I don't. I would like for you to do a search on all the houses that have sold in the last six months and who the cooperating realtors were and then another search on the properties that are currently on the market. I think something fishy is going on in this neighborhood."

"I'll take care of it tomorrow," she replied.

We arrived at the haunted house and paid our entrance fees.

"Now you all understand that we're paying someone to scare us," I said. "I don't want any whining when we get in there."

"No problem," they all said.

We stepped from the lighted entrance into a totally dark hallway. There was a little row of twinkle lights on the floor that we were supposed to follow through the maze.

It's amazing how much total darkness saps the brave right out of you.

I felt Maggie grab my arm and saw Mary take hold of Willie as we started through the maze.

We crept slowly along, expecting the unexpected at any moment, but it never came. Building up the suspense I guessed.

Then suddenly, we heard the roar, the unmistakable sound of a chain saw being fired up, and a guy in one of those goofy white masks that Jason, or somebody, wore in a movie jumped out in front of us.

"Iiiieeeeek!" shouted Mary.

"Ouch!" shouted Willie. "Let go of my arm, you crazy old bat!"

"I think I wet my pants," Mary moaned.

"I think you broke my arm," Willie replied.

So much for 'no problem.'

We went farther into the maze, and as we rounded the corner another figure appeared. He was standing there decapitated with red something oozing out of his neck and holding his head in his arms.

"Oh jeez, Mr. Walt, that's just sick," I heard Willie mutter.

I turned in his direction and almost burst out laughing. I remember watching *Our Gang* and *The Little Rascals* when I was a kid. One of the boys in the gang was Buckwheat. His eyes would get as big as saucers when he was scared. I looked at Willie, and with his dark skin in the pitch-black room, all I saw was two eyes as big as pie plates.

We eased our way forward, very carefully watching for what we would be coming our way next.

But it came from behind us.

We heard something growl and turned to see a figure directly behind us with a big, hairy werewolf mask. His snout protruded with sharp-looking fangs dripping with red blood.

Mary was the closest, and without any hesitation, she punched the poor werewolf right in his snout.

Whack!

"Jesus, lady!" the kid screamed, grabbing his nose. "What's the matter with you?"

"I've had enough of this," Mary wailed. "I'm out of here." She pushed forward into the dark.

"Wait, Mary!" I yelled. "You don't know where you are going."

"I know I'm going to get out of here!" she yelled back. "Hey, here's a door. I'm going through."

The door Mary had opened was, of course, off the lighted trail we were supposed to follow. I just hoped it would take us out.

I heard shuffling ahead as Mary groped her way through the dark room. Whump! Oof!

"Damn! I tripped over something," Mary wailed. "Oh crap! I think it's another one of their dead bodies. They got them everywhere!"

Just then I found a light switch and flicked it on. Sure enough, it was a dead body.

Doris!

We were all speechless as the impact of this horror sank in.

I looked at Willie and saw a tear slide down his wrinkled cheek.

I called it in, and soon The House from Hell was filled with detectives and the crime lab.

It was an hour before we were released and headed for home.

I dropped off Mary and Willie and headed to Maggie's apartment on the Plaza.

Wow, what an evening. We were both on edge after our gruesome discovery.

I walked Maggie to her door, and as she entered, I noticed a bowl of candy on her coffee table.

"Hey, this is good stuff," I said. "You would have been a number one on our hit list."

I pulled out a bag of M&M's and tore it open.

"Oh, that's my favorite," Maggie said. "See, they made them just for me. M&M, Maggie McBride."

"Not so fast," I said, and I turned it upside down. "W&W for Walter Williams."

"Pretty clever," she said and put an M&M between her lips. "You want to come over here and try one?"

I did, and soon we were on our way to Candyland. I took my *Sweet Tart* by the hand and led her into the bedroom.

I tried to get her bra undone but finally had to have some help. I've always been a *Butterfinger*.

I pulled her close to me and nibbled on her neck. That got me a couple of *Snickers*.

I pulled the covers down, and we took a *Tootsie Roll* into bed.

I heard a *Krackel* and *Crunch* and realized it was just my old joints.

I gave her a big *Hershey's Kiss*, and she pulled me close to her.

Then I slipped *Mr. Goodbar Twix* her legs, and we took a heavenly trip down the *MilkyWay*.

When we finished, our hearts were filled with *Almond Joy.*

CHAPTER 3

The next morning we gathered in the squad room, and Captain Short brought us up to date on Doris's murder. She had been killed by a gunshot wound to the back of her head. It had all the earmarks of an execution.

There was very little blood at the scene, indicating that the fatal shot from a .38 had taken place somewhere else and then the body was transported to the haunted house. Of course, no weapon was found at the scene, and so far, forensics had turned up no evidence as to the identity of the killer.

The old warehouse had been rented by a fraternity from UMKC that had set up the haunted house as a fund-raising project. The building itself was owned by L&M Enterprises Inc. The partners of L&M were Salvatore Lorenzo and Emile Mancuso. It was common knowledge that these two characters had ties to the mob and their legitimate businesses were merely fronts for the mob's seamy operations.

The captain said that it was going to be difficult to tie L&M to the murder since the warehouse had been open to the public and hundreds of people had access to it.

I shared with the squad what I had learned from Maxine and Louie the Lip about Joey Piccolo's visit and his warning to each of them. Officers from the northeast patrol said that Piccolo was known to be muscle for the mob.

We all agreed that Piccolo was as good a place as any to start, and a team was assembled to bring him in for questioning. The records division had an address for Piccolo on Garfield. Since Piccolo was a suspected hit man, the tactical unit was given the assignment to bring him in. Ox and I were backup and waited in the street as the tactical boys converged on his apartment.

As we waited by our black and white, we were approached by an old man in coveralls. "If you guys are looking for Joey, he ain't there. He hightailed it out of here about twenty minutes ago. Looked like somebody had lit his ass on fire."

So much for our first lead.

The tactical squad returned to the station, and Ox and I were assigned to stay in the neighborhood and keep an eye on his building and to call it in if he returned.

He never showed.

That evening I went to Maggie's apartment. She had called and told me she had done the research on the Multiple Listing System that I had requested and had some very interesting results.

The Multiple Listing System is an online function of the Greater Kansas City Board of Realtors. Virtually all of the major companies and most of the mom and pop companies are members.

When a company takes a listing, it is posted on the MLS and is available to be seen by all other MLS members. When the listing sells, the pertinent information on the sale, including the names of the cooperating companies, is archived and available to members as well.

I had asked Maggie to track sales in our target area for the last six months and print a list of properties currently on the market.

Maggie handed me the list. "This is a real eye-opener," she said. "One company, Riverfront Realty, is responsible for 90 percent of the sales in the last six months and currently has twenty-five listings in the area."

In my selling days, I had heard of Riverfront Realty but had never sold one of their properties. They were a small firm that primarily concentrated on the northeast Kansas City area.

We booted up Maggie's computer and pulled up the members' page of the MLS. We scrolled through the companies until we found Riverfront Realty and clicked on it. The name of the principal broker popped up.

Michael Lorenzo!

The only other licensed associate in the company was Constance Lorenzo.

It didn't take a Sam Spade to figure out that Michael Lorenzo of Riverfront Realty and Salvatore Lorenzo of L&M Enterprises were probably related.

I looked at the list of past sales in the area, and it was no surprise that almost all of them were double-dippers. Riverfront Realty was both the listing and selling company.

Unfortunately, the MLS archives don't record the names of the buyers of the properties, so we pulled up Jackson County Information Service on the computer.

In this program, you can enter a person's name, and all the property he owns will be displayed, or conversely you can enter a property address, and the name of the property owner will be displayed.

We randomly selected one of the sold properties and entered the address. The owner's name was Eastside Properties Inc.

I entered Eastside Properties in the computer and bingo! Forty-five tracts popped up!

So far, our detective work had discovered that the building where Doris's body was found was owned by L&M Enterprises. The broker at Riverfront Realty was tied to L&M, so both likely had ties to the mob.

Riverfront Realty had made a bazillion sales in the area to Eastside Properties and currently had twenty-five active listings.

The mob had strongly suggested to the local hookers and drug dealers that they should relocate.

Obviously, something big was going on in the area. But what?

The next obvious step was to find out who the principal partners of Eastside Properties Inc. were. We didn't know how to do that.

I would take our findings to Captain Short and let the experts do some digging.

I kissed Maggie good-bye, thanked her for her detective work, and drove home.

When I arrived, Willie was waiting for me on the front porch.

"Hey, Mr. Walt. You heard anything from Milton in de las few days?"

"No, I haven't seen him, but I've been pretty preoccupied."

"Well, I ain't seen him either, and I think we oughta check on him."

Eighty-seven-year-old Milton Shapiro was my tenant in 3-B. He had been with me about fifteen years. He was a sweet old guy who minded his own business and was never a bother.

We climbed the stairs to the third floor and knocked on Milton's door.

No answer.

It was nine o'clock in the evening, so we knew he should be home. I knocked again.

No answer.

I went to my apartment across the hall and retrieved the key to 3-B from my key safe.

I slipped the key in the lock and pushed the door open a crack. "Milton, you home?" I called.

No answer.

I pushed the door open and flipped on the light. Milton was sitting in his easy chair with his newspaper on his lap.

He was dead.

"Oh my Lord," Willie wailed. "Ole Milton has done gone an' left us!"

I called 911, and soon the medical examiner and an EMT vehicle arrived.

In the interval between my call and their arrival, the other tenants in the building gathered outside the door. Most of my tenants had been with me for ten years or more and had become close friends.

As the professor looked in at Milton sitting upright in his chair, he remarked, "Death is peaceful. It's often the transition that's troublesome. But it looks like it wasn't too troublesome for our old friend. We can only hope the same for the rest of us."

The medical examiner ruled that it was a death from natural causes, and the EMTs placed the body on a gurney and wheeled it out.

As Milton passed by eighty-three-year-old Bernice Crenshaw from 2-B, she leaned and whispered, "Good-bye, Milton. I'll be seeing you soon."

We had all lost a good friend.

The next morning I sat down with Captain Short and shared what Maggie and I had learned from the Multiple Listing Service. I told him I would like to nose around the neighborhood and see if could find out why all the properties were on the market. He agreed, and Ox and I were on our way.

We drove up and down the streets in the blocks from Holmes to Troost. The bulk of the "for sale" signs were in this area.

The neighborhood was old, and most of the houses had already seen better days, but we pulled up in front of one home that had obviously seen better care. A Riverfront Realty sign was in the front yard.

One of the cardinal rules of real estate is that you never talk directly to a seller who is listed with another agent. If you do and get caught, you're in deep doodoo.

But I wasn't an agent anymore. I'm a cop.

We went to the door and knocked. A gray-haired gentleman in his sixties answered the door, and his wife stood behind him peering out.

"My name is Walt Williams, and this is my partner, George Wilson. We're with the Kansas City Police Department." I held my badge where they could see it.

"How can we help you?"

"Do you mind if we come in? We'd like to visit with you about what's happening in your neighborhood."

They looked at each other for a moment, and he said, "Sure, come on in."

They introduced themselves as Mr. and Mrs. Lawrence. They had lived in the house for fifteen years and had seen many changes take place in the neighborhood.

"How did you happen to decide that you wanted to sell your home?" I asked.

"We hadn't really thought about it much," he replied, "until the real estate lady came by and talked to us. She asked if we had seen all the other homes for sale in the area, and, of course, we had. Then she asked if we had noticed the houses that had been boarded up.

"She told us that the property values in the area were going down rapidly. And if we ever wanted to get anything out of our home, we'd better do it fast."

Oh boy!

This is a practice in the real estate industry known as blockbusting, and it's illegal.

In neighborhoods where a transition is taking place, like when one ethnic group is being replaced by another or when businesses are encroaching on a residential area, it is a violation of the realtor code of ethics to approach homeowners and attempt to scare them into selling.

If you get caught, you can lose your license.

"So basically you were frightened into listing your home for sale?" I asked.

"Yes, I guess you could say that."

"How has it gone for you so far? Are you getting any showings on your home?"

"We haven't had a one, and we've lowered the price twice already."

At that moment there was a knock on the door. Mr. Lawrence opened the door, and Connie Lorenzo huffed into the room.

"I know who you are!" she bellowed. "You're Walter Williams with City Wide Realty! What are you doing talking to my sellers? I'm going to report you to the Board of Realtors!"

"Whoa, Connie. You'd better back off for a minute. You're only half right. I'm Walter Williams, but I haven't been with City Wide for almost a year." I held up my badge. "After visiting with Mr. and Mrs. Lawrence, it would appear that you're the one who's going to be reported to the board for blockbusting. Any comment?"

"You don't have any idea who you're dealing with here, Williams." She snarled. "You're in way over your head."

"We'll see. Especially after we interview a few more of your listings. I think you are going to have some explaining to do."

She turned and stormed out the door.

We thanked the Lawrences and told them someone else from the department might be contacting them.

As soon as I left the house, I called Maggie on her cell.

"I need another favor," I said. "Could you go back into the MLS and do a history search on the homes purchased by Eastside Properties? Pay particular attention to days on the market and any price reductions."

"Will do," she replied.

Ox and I interviewed three other sellers of homes listed with Riverfront Realty, each with the same results. Each one had been approached by Connie Lorenzo, and after she had frightened them with tales of plummeting property values, they listed, hoping to salvage something from their lifelong investment.

And, as with the Lawrence family, prices had been dropped after months with no showings.

Maggie called back and said that all of the properties purchased by Eastside had been on the market for at least 180 days, and most had sold for close to half of their original list price.

A scam for sure.

But who was behind it?

We reported back to Captain Short and gave him the information we had gleaned.

I had hoped that by this time we would know who the principal owners of Eastside Properties Inc. were, but Shorty said that they had discovered Eastside was just a shell corporation owned by a larger corporation that was operating out of the Bahamas.

Dead end.

We clocked out, and I headed home.

When I arrived home, four strangers were waiting for me on the porch.

"Hello, Mr. Williams? I'm Gloria, and this is my sister, Shirley, and these are our husbands. We're Milton Shapiro's daughters."

"So nice to meet you," I replied. "I'm so sorry for your loss. Milton was a really good friend. We're going to miss him. Have you come a long way?"

"Not really," she replied. "We live in Overland Park, Kansas, about forty-five minutes from here."

"Hmm, I don't recall seeing you here before. When was the last time you saw Milton?"

"Oh, gee, I guess it's been about two years since we've seen Dad. Isn't that about right, Shirley?"

"Yeah, that sounds about right," she replied. "I think we dropped by after a Chiefs game one Sunday, but he wasn't home."

"Oh yeah, I remember now. Anyway, we brought a pick-up truck and thought we would start loading some of Daddy's stuff if you'll let us in."

Oh boy! The vultures had landed.

"Hang on here a minute," I said. "I'll be right back."

I had totally forgotten that Milton had given me an envelope several years ago. He told me to keep it somewhere safe and open it when he died. I had put it in my safe and forgotten about it until then.

I retrieved the envelope and returned to the front porch.

I explained to Gloria and Shirley what Milton had requested, and they watched as I opened the envelope.

Inside was another sealed envelope, and written on the outside were the words "The Last Will and Testament of Milton Shapiro. To be opened by my attorney, Oswald Meachum."

"Well, I guess that settles it," I said. "Obviously Milton has some specific instructions as to the settlement of his estate, so I guess we'll just have to wait until we hear from his attorney."

"So we came all this way and you're not going to let us in?" Gloria whined.

"You got that right," I said and left them standing on the porch.

I was met in the front hall by my long-term tenant, the professor. "Dreadful people!" he said. "They came to my door asking which apartment was Milton's. Just imagine! They live a mere forty-five minutes away, and to my knowledge, they've never been to see him. Disgraceful!"

"I agree," I said. "And here they are, on the doorstep ready to haul away his stuff and he's barely dead."

"It's people like them that make me want to recite the 'Senility Prayer.'"

"Don't you mean the 'Serenity Prayer'?" I asked.

"That one would certainly apply too, but I think the 'Senility Prayer' is more apropos in this situation:

God, grant me the senility
To forget the people
I don't like
The good fortune
To run into the ones I do
And the eyesight
To tell the difference.

"Amen to that," I said.

I had reached the second floor, and Bernice Crenshaw met me in the hall. I guessed she had been watching out the window.

I had been worried about Bernice. She had taken Milton's inevitable death pretty hard.

"How're you feeling, Bernice?"

"I'm doing better now. Would you like to come in for a minute? I have something to show you."

She went to a bookshelf and brought back an old leather bound book.

"Milton loaned this to me about a week before he passed. It's his favorite book of poems. What should I do with it now?"

"I think Milton would love for you to keep it to remember him by," I replied.

Bernice had one of those small Yamaha electronic pianos against the wall. There was a crystal bowl sitting on top of it filled with water, and a strange object was floating in the liquid.

I took a closer look and was shocked to see that the floater was a condom.

"Bernice, what in the world are you doing with this?"

"Oh, yes," she replied. "Isn't it wonderful? I was walking down Armour Boulevard a few weeks ago and found this little package. It said to put it on your organ and keep it wet and it would prevent disease. I don't have an organ, so I put it on my piano, and I think it's working. I haven't been sick since!"

A miracle of modern medicine!

"Sit!" Emile Mancuso ordered. "I want a full report on our project. Connie, are you getting any static from the homeowners?"

"Not really. The board-ups and vacant buildings have put a scare into them. Everyone's eager to get out as quickly as they can and salvage as much equity as possible. Eastside Properties has already closed on dozens of parcels and we have listings on most of the rest. We're just biding time until they lower their asking prices. But --- there is one problem."

"Spit it out."

"A cop, Walt Williams. I found him at one of my listings questioning my seller. Walt was a realtor for thirty years. I know he suspects that something is fishy. His girlfriend is still with City Wide Realty. I just hope they don't become a problem."

"Keep your eye on him, Connie. Let me know if we need to have Joey pay him a visit."

Mancuso turned to his hit man. "Anything to report, Joey?"

"No problems so far, Emile. I had one hooker that wouldn't listen to reason. When she was found with a slug in the back of her head the rest of the whores and druggies split.

"Most of the businesses have listened to reason, but we still have a few hold-outs, The Cozy Corner, that gay joint at Twelfth and Troost, an old boarded up warehouse on Harrison and the Blue Moon on

Twelfth. I'm workin' on them, but I may have to do some arm twisting."

"Do what you gotta do. Sal, is your cop playin' ball?"

"Just got a tip from him this morning. The Drug Enforcement Unit is planning a hit on that old warehouse where we're storing the last shipment of drugs from Mexico."

"Perfect! Joey, get some of the boys and move the stuff out of there. Looks like things are coming together. I just hope, for his sake, that the councilman is getting his part of the deal done."

CHAPTER 4

Apparently our detective work had generated some interest at the precinct.

At the squad meeting the next morning, Captain Short said that the captains of the various squads had met to discuss any unusual activity that each might have encountered in the area.

The captain of the Drug Unit had shared that they had been following a lead on drug activity in the northeast area and had a tip that a large quantity of drugs was being stored in an old abandoned storefront building on Twelfth Street owned by L&M Enterprises.

If there was really a connection between L&M and Eastside Properties, it was possible that the money to purchase the properties was coming from the drug trade.

A raid by the tactical squad was organized, and as before, Ox and I were assigned to stand by on the perimeter and keep citizens away from the storefront during the raid.

The tactical squad surrounded the building, front and back, and we heard the crash as the metal battering ram burst through the door.

Silence.

The squad leader emerged from the building shaking his head.

The building was empty.

Everyone was perplexed. The lead had come from a source that was usually quite reliable.

Ox and I were assigned to interview neighboring businesses to check on activity at the storefront.

After visiting with several shop owners surrounding the storefront, we came up empty. No one had seen any activity there, at least during normal business hours.

We were heading back to our black and white when I glanced down an alley and saw a homeless guy leaned up against the wall with a bottle in a brown paper bag.

If this guy lived there in the alley, he might have seen something during the wee hours of the morning.

"Excuse me, sir. We'd like to ask you some questions." I showed him my badge.

"Whadda you want?"

"Have you seen any activity in that storefront during the night?"

"Maybe I have and maybe I haven't." He held up the sack with his bottle. "I just might need a little something extra to help my memory along."

Great!

I looked at Ox, and he shrugged his shoulders.

I pulled out a twenty and waved it in front of the bum. "How's your memory now?"

"It's gettin' better. I seem to recall a big truck pullin' up to the front of that building about two o'clock this morning. They was packin' stuff out for about an hour, and then they left." He snatched the twenty out of my hand.

"Did you recognize anyone?"

"Maybe I did and maybe I didn't."

I pulled out another twenty.

"Joey Piccolo and three of his goons were loadin' the truck." He snatched the second twenty.

I called the information back to Captain Short, and we continued our canvass of the neighborhood.

Just after lunch, I received a call on my cell phone. It was Oswald Meachum. I had dropped Milton's will by the attorney's office on my way to work.

"Walt, would you be available to meet at my office at four o'clock? I'd like to go over Milton's will."

"Sure, I think I can get off an hour early."

"Oh, and bring Willie Duncan with you too."

I picked up Willie, and we went to Oswald Meachum's law office on Broadway. When we arrived, Gloria and Shirley were already in the conference room. We acknowledged one another and took our seats as Meachum entered the room.

"I've reviewed Milton's will, and everything seems to be in order. I'll read the provisions of the will and Milton's last request, and then I'll take any questions you may have.

"To my friend and landlord, Walter Williams, I leave the contents of my apartment. You may keep the items, sell them, or donate them to charity as you see fit.

"To my good friend Willie Duncan, I leave the sum of $5,000 for all the assistance he has given me over the years.

"To my daughters Gloria and Shirley, I leave one dollar each and wish each of them a happy life.

The remainder of my estate I leave to the Thomas Swope Senior Center.

"It is my last request that I be cremated and my ashes spread over the parking lot at the Overland Park Mall. That way I will be assured that my daughters will visit me at least twice a week.

"Signed: Milton Shapiro."

Silence.

No one stirred for several moments, and finally Gloria and Shirley rose and stomped out the door without a word.

"Well, that was awkward," I said.

"Awkward, yes, but definitely just," Meachum replied.

Ah yes, Lady Justice.

She turns up at the most unexpected places.

As we drove home I asked Willie what he planned to do with his good fortune.

Without hesitation, he replied, "Doris didn' have no family, so I'se gonna give her a real good funeral and put her to rest proper."

The Lord works in mysterious ways.

The next day as we were cruising the neighborhood of our target area, we saw a wisp of smoke coming from a small warehouse building on Harrison Street.

We pulled up in front of the building just as flames burst through the ground floor windows.

Ox called it in, and I ran to the front door. I tried it and found it unlocked. I eased the door open just a crack and saw that the blaze was concentrated in the back of the building.

I pulled my handkerchief, covered my nose and mouth, and entered the building.

I saw a body on the floor near a flaming wall. I pointed to the body as Ox joined me in the room, and together we pulled it into the street as fire trucks, with sirens blaring, arrived on the scene.

Ox and I stared at the dead man and realized at the same time that this was the old drunk we had questioned in the alley the day before.

He had suffered a gunshot wound to the back of the head just like Doris, and then we noticed something protruding from the corner of his mouth.

I gently pried his lips apart and saw two twenty-dollar bills stuffed in his mouth.

Our questioning had gotten him killed.

I had noticed a sticker on the door that said, "In case of emergency, call 1–816–555–1357." I dialed the number, and a man answered.

"This is Walter Williams, Kansas City Police Department. Are you the owner of a small warehouse on Harrison?"

"Yes, this is Ivor Polinski. I am the owner. Is something wrong?"

I told him about the fire, and he said he could be on the scene in ten minutes.

In less than ten minutes, a blue Lincoln Town Car pulled up, and a tall, gray-haired man in his fifties stepped out.

"Mr. Polinski? I'm Walt Williams. I called you."

He stood on the curb staring at the warehouse now engulfed in flames, and a tear rolled down his cheek.

"This is all I had left from my father," he said. "He bought this business when he came to America from the old country, and with it, he made a life for us here."

"I'm so sorry," I said. "Do you have any idea how the fire might have started?"

"No. No one has used the building for years, but I just couldn't get rid of it even though I have had offers."

That got my attention.

"Tell me about your offers," I said.

"A woman from Riverfront Realty has approached me several times. She said that she had a buyer interested in the property who would pay cash. But I told her I just couldn't part with it yet. She was quite insistent, but I still said no."

Hmm! A holdout right in the middle of an area being acquired by a dummy corporation suddenly catches on fire.

Definitely a connection.

Several days had passed without any breaks in the case, and we were all very frustrated.

The homeless man had been shot with the same gun that had killed Doris, and an accelerant had been found at the fire scene, but there was no new evidence that could link these crimes to either Joey Piccolo or Eastside Properties.

I had received a call from Oswald Meachum saying that I was free to dispose of Milton's belongings as I saw fit. I rounded up the other tenants in the building who were close to Milton, and we went through his things a piece at a time. Each one found a few treasures that they wanted to keep to remind them of Milton. The clothing we boxed up and sent to the Salvation Army.

Milton's furniture, while old, was in excellent condition, so I decided I would leave it in the apartment for the time being and possibly rent the unit furnished.

In addition to my apartment and Willie's kitchenette in the basement, there are five other units in the building. All of my other tenants have been with me at least ten years. Since I have to live with whomever I rent to, I am very picky when it comes to choosing new tenants.

I can only be choosy about whom I rent to if I don't advertise.

Once I run an ad in the newspaper for a two-bedroom apartment, all of the anti-discrimination laws come into play, and I can find myself stuck with someone I don't want as my neighbor. I would rather leave a unit empty while I wait for someone to come along who I think would fit in with our little group.

The apartment had only been ready to go about a week when I received a call from Oscar Evans, an old friend and fellow landlord.

The grapevine travels fast.

"Hey, Walt, I heard you might have an apartment available in your Armour building."

"Might have," I replied suspiciously. "So what?"

"So I've got just the tenant for you. I know how picky you are, and this guy would fit in perfectly with your old-timers over there."

"Okay, give me the scoop."

"His name is Jerry Singer. He is seventy-two years old and retired, of course. He has been with me for seven years and never even been late with a rent payment."

"If he's so great, why give him to me?"

"If I had a vacancy I'd move him in a minute, but I'm full. I just sold the building where he lives, and the new owners want to convert it back to a single family, so all the tenants have to go. You'll love him."

"Yeah, I'll bet."

I took the information on Jerry Singer and did my usual due diligence. I ran his name through

51

casenet.com, and no one had filed a lawsuit against him. I ran him through police records, and he hadn't even had a parking ticket.

So far, so good.

I gave Singer a call and asked him to come by the building for an interview. He was right on time for the interview, and I invited him into my unit.

The minute I laid eyes on him, my mind went back about forty years, and the image of Wally Cox as Mr. Peepers came to mind.

He was about five feet, four inches tall and couldn't have weighed more than 125 pounds. He wore big, round glasses and a black bow tie. Wide plaid suspenders held up his baggy breeches, which was fortunate because he had no ass. It looked like he had traded butts with a grasshopper.

I had asked the professor to sit in with us. I really respect his insight and wisdom, and I know that he is an excellent judge of character.

I made the introductions and launched into my usual grilling of prospective tenants. He said all the right things.

Finally, I said, "How's your health? Are there any physical problems we should be aware of?"

"I do pretty well for an old guy," he replied. "When I get up each day, I get the newspaper and read the obituaries. If my name's not there I figure the Good Lord's given me another day, and I carry on."

I looked at the professor, and he gave me a little nod.

"Well, Jerry," I said as I handed him a key, "looks like we're going to be neighbors."

He took the key, signed the lease, wrote a check for the rent and deposit, and left whistling a jaunty tune.

"Nice man," said the professor. "He has a good attitude and a sense of humor."

We found out soon enough how prophetic that was.

We still had no leads in our murder and arson cases. The only tie we had to real people was Riverfront Realty. We knew they had to be involved, but so far, the only thing we could pin on them was the blockbusting, and that wasn't a police matter. It was a license violation.

The task force thought that by putting pressure on Riverfront Realty we might smoke out others involved in the scheme, so they asked Ox and I to pursue a complaint with the Missouri Real Estate Commission.

I met with David Richards, my old friend and broker of City Wide Realty. I shared with him what I had learned about Riverfront Realty's activities in our target area. He agreed that this was a classic example of blockbusting.

We reviewed the Missouri statutes and printed the appropriate complaint forms from their Web site.

Then the work began.

The complaints had to come from the sellers themselves, so our job was to go back to each seller, explain the complaint process, and hope they weren't too intimidated to follow through.

We started with Mr. and Mrs. Lawrence. They were skeptical at first, but after I showed them the statistics on Riverfront Realty's previous sales, they were incensed at the underhanded practices of the company.

We had spent an hour going over the forms, and the Lawrences were ready to sign when we heard a crash. A brick came sailing through the front window. We all ducked for cover, but when nothing else followed we picked ourselves up and examined the brick. A note was attached that read, "Watch your step or your place will end up like Polinski's."

Naturally, the Lawrences were intimidated and refused to sign the complaint.

I couldn't really blame them.

Ox and I retreated to our car and found the back tire punctured and a note under the windshield wiper.

"Back off, old man, or you'll wind up like Doris!"

That's the kind of note that will get your attention.

I returned home that evening exhausted, frustrated, and a little apprehensive. As I entered the foyer, I met Jerry.

"Hey, Walt. What does a seventy-five-year-old woman have between her breasts that a twenty-five-year-old doesn't? Her navel!"

He bent over double, laughing.

Well, okay then. That was unusual.

I went upstairs to my apartment and remembered that I had forgotten to get my mail, so I trudged back to the foyer. Jerry was still there, and as he saw me, his eyes lit up.

"Hey, Walt. I was talking to a friend the other day. He said he had it all—money, a beautiful house, a big car, the love of a beautiful woman, and then bam! It was all gone."

"Gosh, that's awful. What happened?" I asked.

"His wife found out."

Oh no. This can't be good.

I got my mail, and when I returned to my apartment, Willie was waiting outside my door.

"Mr. Walt, I gotta talk to you," he said, and he stepped inside and closed the door.

"What's up?"

"It's dat new guy! He's drivin' me crazy. Evva time I steps out of my apartment, he's on me wif some dumb joke. What's dat all about?"

"Well, it seems our new tenant thinks he's a stand-up comedian. I've been getting the same thing."

"Well, if he don' quit it, I'm gonna have to bust him in de mouf and see if he tinks dat's funny."

"Let's not resort to violence. Let me see what I can do."

Willie left, and I called Oscar Evans.

"Hey, Oscar, Walt here. What's the deal with Jerry Singer?"

"Oh, you mean Jerry the Joker," he replied.

"So you knew all along! How could you do this to me?"

"Hey, I didn't lie to you. Everything I said about Jerry was true. I, uh, just didn't tell you everything I knew. Anyway, you checked him out for yourself."

"God will get you for this, Oscar!"

"Not if he gets you first," he replied, and I heard him snicker as he hung up.

I walked out of my apartment door, and Jerry was standing in the hall.

"Hey, Walt. I'll bet you didn't know that my wife and I were happy for twenty years."

"No, Jerry, I didn't know that."

"Yeah, then we met."

Great, I'd rented an apartment to Rodney Dangerfield.

I hustled down the stairs and was met by the professor.

"I think we may have a problem," he said.

"No kidding?"

"Yes indeed. Jerry approached me this morning and said he had a philosophical issue he would like to discuss with me. I was delighted to have someone with whom to ponder the mysteries of life. Then he said, 'If corn oil is made from corn and vegetable oil is made from vegetables, then what is baby oil made from?'"

"Sorry about that, Professor. I'll see what I can do."

56

I gotta get out of here, I thought and headed out the door. Jerry was waiting in the hallway.

"Hey, Walt, you were a real estate agent. I've got a good one for you."

He told it as we walked out to the car.

I jumped in the car and called Maggie.

"I hope you're home," I said. "I've had a tough day. Someone's threatened to shoot me, and I've rented an apartment to Rodney Dangerfield."

Maggie greeted me with a big kiss, handed me a glass of Arbor Mist, and sat me down on the couch.

"Okay, tell me all about it," she said.

So I did.

When I finished with my tale of woe, I said, "Oh, I've got a good one from Jerry you can use with your next client. Knock, knock."

"Who's there?"

"Amaryllis."

"Amaryllis who?"

"Amaryllis state agent. Do you want to buy a house?"

She gave me the look.

All guys know about 'the look.' It is a phenomenon that is exclusive to women of all ages. It is invoked when you misbehave. You get it first from your mother.

Fathers can threaten, scold, and even spank, but none of these can generate the fear of 'the look.' With Dad, you know what's coming, but the look causes visions of unspeakable things in your imagination that are just too horrible to comprehend.

If words accompany the look, they are spoken sternly and with great authority. Even proper names come under its purview.

When I was a kid, the boy who lived next door was called Bobby by everyone, but when he was in trouble, first came the look and then, "Robert Lee, you come here this instant."

And he came.

Wives and girlfriends have it too.

Do they attend some kind of class, or is it an inborn trait like the swallows flying back to Capistrano?

Of course, when wives or girlfriends give the look, there is the threat of even greater punishment than a mother could ever inflict.

You guys know what I mean.

Then the look softened, and she said, "I think I've got an idea." She grabbed the newspaper.

She looked at her watch and said, "Let's go. We've got to hurry."

I didn't argue.

We hustled back to my building, and I knocked on Jerry's door. "Come on. Get your jacket. We're going for a ride."

We drove to Broadway and parked in front of a storefront building with a flashing neon sign that said, "Kansas City Comedy Club."

I paid our entrance fees, and we took a table close to the front. Jerry was excited as he sat and listened to the comedian on stage.

When the guy had finished, there was a smattering of applause, and Jerry whispered to me, "He really wasn't that funny for a professional."

"He wasn't a professional. Tonight is amateur night. And guess what? You're on in fifteen minutes."

His eyes got as big as saucers, and his bow tie bobbed up and down on his throat. "Me? I get to go up there?"

"You sure do. Now make the most of it."

When Jerry's turn came, he boldly strode to the stage and took the mike.

"As I look around the room, I see mostly young people. You really don't know what you're in for. We senior citizens have a whole set of problems that you can't even imagine.

"Why, just yesterday, I went to the doctor and told him I wanted my sex drive lowered. 'Jerry,' he said, 'you're seventy-two years old. Don't you think your sex drive is all in your head?'

"'You're damn right it is,' I told him. 'That's why I want it lowered.'"

A roar went up from the crowd.

"I have a friend, Morris," Jerry continued. "He went to the doctor to get a physical. A few days later the doc saw Morris walking down the street with a gorgeous young woman on his arm, and the doctor said, 'Morris, what in the world are you doing?'

"'Just doing what you said, Doc. "Get a hot mama and be cheerful."'"

"'No, I didn't say that! I said, "You've got a heart murmur. Be careful! And don't you realize that hitting on a young thing like that could be dangerous?'

"'Hey,' Morris replied, 'if she dies, she dies.'"

Another roar went up from the crowd. I gave Jerry a thumbs-up, and he gave me a wink.

I thought maybe we had solved our problem.

CHAPTER 5

Ox and I were patrolling the Northeast neighborhood and had just pulled onto Twelfth Street. An old black gentleman, obviously distraught, was waving to us.

Ox pulled to the curb and rolled down his window. "Calm down, old-timer. What's going on?"

He pointed to the door of The Blue Room Jazz Club. "It's Spats. Must be somethin' wrong. The door's locked and he's always there this time of mornin'."

"Spats? Who's that?"

"Orville! Orville Johnson. Everybody calls him Spats. He owns The Blue Room. We all get together for coffee every mornin'."

"Maybe he just overslept," Ox offered. "Did you try to call him?"

"Sho did. Called his house and called the Club, but he ain't answering. It ain't like him. I know somethin's wrong."

"We'll take a look"

Ox tried the door but it was locked. I squinted through the leaded glass in the door. Total darkness inside.

"Sir," Ox said, "please stay right here. My partner and I will check around back."

We circled around through the alley. An old pick-up was parked next to the building.

Ox tried the back door and found it unlocked.

We pulled our service weapons and stepped into the darkness.

"Mr. Johnson? It's the police."

Nothing but silence.

I felt along the wall and located the light switch.

A bare bulb hanging from the ceiling came on, casting an eerie glow on the body of an elderly man lying in a pool of blood.

"Damn!" Ox muttered. "I'm guessing that's our missing Spats. Looks like he took one to the back of the head, just like Doris and the homeless guy."

"I'll call it in," I replied. "You check the rest of the place and make sure we're alone."

After the scene was secure, we headed back to the front of the building.

"Sir," Ox began. "By the way, what's your name?"

"Benny. Benny Burton. Did you find Spats? Is everything okay?"

"I'm sorry to have to be the bearer of bad news, but yes, we found your friend. I'm afraid he's dead."

Benny slumped onto the step. "I knew it! I jus' knew dat somethin' bad was gonna happen. Spats was a stubborn old cuss. I told him he should sell, but he just wouldn't listen."

"So someone's been trying to buy the club?"

"Yep, some woman has been around two or three times. Says she's got an investor that will pay cash, but Spats didn't want no part of it."

"Why not?"

"Spats has owned this old place for over forty years. Bought it back when Kansas City Jazz was the

62

hottest thing around. He played a mean sax. Heck, I played the drums, but I never was in Spats league. Some of the finest jazz musicians in the country played this old joint. Just too many memories here. Spats wasn't ready to give the place up."

Just then, the detectives from homicide and the CSI guys pulled up.

Ox and I were sent off to keep the growing crowd of looky-lous away from the crime scene.

Three hours later, the body of poor Spats was on its way to the morgue, the detectives had finished with the scene and we were sent on our merry way.

As we headed back to the precinct, I noticed a sign in the yard of one of the homes that Riverside Realty had listed. It was announcing an auction the next day. The owners apparently had found a buyer and were liquidating their personal belongings.

It occurred to me that this might be an opportunity to quiz the owners without being too obvious. I also remembered that Maggie loved to go to auctions. Since I was scheduled to be off the next day, I gave my sweetie a call.

She was thrilled.

Maggie lives in an apartment near the Country Club Plaza. I picked her up, and we headed to Mel's Diner for breakfast.

Mel's is my favorite place to eat. Maggie's, not so much.

Maggie is into salads and quiches and steamed vegetables.

I'm more into sugar, grease and meat.

You can get all of that at Mel's, but he specializes in the sugar, grease and meat. And you never go away hungry.

I was enjoying a huge platter of biscuits covered with white cream gravy and a steaming mug of coffee, and Maggie was picking at a veggie omelet and sipping green tea.

"Walt," she said, "I know you're not a big fan of auctions. There's more to this visit than just rummaging around through boxes of crap."

"You got me. These folks, the Greens, are clients of Riverside Realty. I thought I might get the inside scoop on their sale."

"I understand, but leave me out of that part. If Connie Lorenzo sees me anywhere close to her sellers, she'll be on me like a duck on a June bug."

"No problem. I'll talk to them while you're picking through their stuff."

We turned onto Ninth Street almost three blocks from the Green property. Cars and pickup trucks were already lined up bumper to bumper along the street. We squeezed into a parking spot and walked the three blocks to the auction.

Wall-to-wall people.

Long flatbed trailers had been parked in the yard and were covered with the smaller items, and furniture was lined along the driveway. Two trailers were billowing smoke, and the scent of grilled hot dogs and fried funnel cakes drifted our way.

Now right there are two food items that define the paradox of human consumption. They are probably filled with stuff that gives you diabetes, cancer, gout, and who knows what, but they taste so damn good!

On the other hand, you have broccoli and cauliflower, which supposedly cure all of the above, but they taste like crap.

There's simply no justice in that.

Wouldn't it be great if broccoli tasted like hot dogs, grilled brown and skin cracked with the fat dripping out, and cauliflower tasted like a funnel cake covered with strawberry jam and powdered sugar? And vice versa. Everyone would be much healthier.

A big, old golden retriever was busy roaming through the crowd getting pats on the head. I wondered if he belonged to the Greens and if so where he was headed. Most apartments or assisted living facilities frown on pets.

Auctions are a strange place. They remind me of the TV newscasts where they show the huge crowd at the New York Stock Exchange and everyone is frantically waving and bidding. You get caught up in the frenzy of the moment.

Same thing here, only on a smaller scale.

You get there early so that you can scout out the items you want to buy, but stuff is sold one piece at a time. You may have to stand around for hours before your item comes up for bid.

Then there's always at least one other person who has coveted the same item, and as the bidding starts, you soon discover who your competition is. As the bid increases, you think, *by golly, I didn't stand here four hours just to let that old biddy get my toaster.*

You wind up spending $28 for a used toaster that you could have bought brand-new for $19.95 at Walmart.

We're a strange breed.

Men come to auctions for two things, tools and guns.

Make that three things—tools, guns, and because their wives said so.

Women like the cute stuff. Maggie is a woman. Therefore, you guessed it.

"Walt, come over here. You just have to see this."

"What am I looking at?"

"This beautiful hand-quilted bedspread. It's a wedding ring pattern."

"So?"

"So I want it!"

"Why?"

"Why? Because it's beautiful; that's why. And I want to hang it on my wall."

"On your wall? Are you nuts?"

Wrong reply.

"Walt, this isn't just a quilt. It's a work of art. Every stitch was made by hand. It probably took hundreds of hours to sew. Don't you get it?"

I didn't get it. It's a guy thing.

Next to the quilt, I saw a box of stringy white things. It looked like a web that had been spun by an albino spider. Then I recognized what they were. I hadn't seen any of them for years. My grandmother used to have them all over the house.

Doilies!

I remember when I visited my grandparents' farm in the late forties and early fifties. There was no such thing as television or the Internet. After supper, we did one of two things; we either played cards or turned on the radio.

The radios in those days, with all their vacuum tubes, were as big as the old console TV's of the sixties. Grandpa would sit in his easy chair and smoke his pipe, I would lie on the floor, and Grandma would sit and crochet doilies as we listened to *Fibber Magee and Mollie* or *Innersanctum*.

That show, with its creepy, creaking door, scared the crap out of me.

Since there wasn't much else to do except listen to the radio and crochet, Grandma had doilies everywhere. Every chair had doilies on both arms in case you forgot to wash when you came in from doing chores and on the headrest in case you put on too much Brylcreem.

Doilies! Where did that name come from? It's a goofy name. Say it really slow and think about it.

Doiiiiillllie.

There are all kinds of weird names.

Who was the guy that saw a four-legged creature for the first time and said, "That's an Aardvark." I'll bet it was some aasshole named Aaron.

They say English is the hardest language to learn. I believe it.

Take words like knuckle, knee, and knob. Why aren't they nuckle, nee, and nob? Okay, so the K is silent. If it's not going to do anything, why bother?

And if knuckle is correct, why not knasty? Some things just don't make sense.

As I was pondering these great mysteries of life, Maggie tugged my arm. "Walt, you've got to go get a number so we can bid."

Great.

I went to the little booth that dispensed numbers. By the time I was finished, I had almost given as much information as when I applied for my Social Security.

The lady handed me the number on a little white card, 666.

Oh no. This couldn't be good.

Now I'm not a religious zealot, nor am I overly superstitious, but everyone knows that the number 666 is the devil's number and carries the mark of the beast, whatever that is.

I'm not Catholic, but I crossed myself, just in case, and went back to Maggie.

The auction was just starting. One by one the articles were held up for viewing by the auctioneer and sold off to the highest bidder.

Maggie whispered in my ear, "There's Mr. and Mrs. Green."

I looked on the porch and saw two eighty-something seniors standing side by side, holding hands.

After thirty years in the real estate business, I had occasion to know many golden-agers who had reached this critical point in their lives. Lying on the flatbeds in front of them were a lifetime of memories, of family members long gone, of children now raised, and of a marriage shared together. All their worldly possessions that they had cherished and saved over the years were laid bare to be whisked away by strangers.

It's not an easy time.

The auctioneer held open a wooden case filled with silverware. My grandma had one just like it. The good stuff only came out on Sundays or when company came by. It had probably been handed down for several generations.

Who uses silverware today? It has to be polished. Busy housewives use stainless that can be thrown in the dishwasher. It sold for five dollars.

As the winning bidder took the wooden box away, I saw Mrs. Green turn into her husband's arms and sob. He held her tight.

"This is my chance," I whispered to Maggie. "Keep an eye out for Connie or Michael Lorenzo."

She nodded and I made my way through the crowd to the porch.

"Mr. and Mrs. Green? My name is Walt Williams,"
I said, holding up my badge. "I'm actually off duty
right now, but I wonder if you'd mind answering a
few questions for me?"

"Oh, my!" Mrs. Green said, obviously alarmed.
"The auctioneer said he'd gotten all the required
permits. Are we in trouble?"

"No, no, nothing like that," I assured her. "I'd just
like to ask you some questions about the sale of your
home. My unit has been monitoring the activity in
your neighborhood and anything you could share
might be helpful."

"Certainly! We always want to cooperate with the
police. What do you want to know?"

"Well, let's start with how long your home was on
the market."

"Going on six months," she replied.

"Did you have to lower the price to get a buyer?"

Mrs. Green looked at her husband and nodded.
"We've been here thirty-three years and kept the
property in good condition. I thought we listed it at a
fair price, but no one came to see it. Our realtor came
by every month or so and told us we'd never get a
buyer unless we lowered our price. We just kept
cutting and cutting until it was almost what we paid
for it thirty-three years ago."

"I don't suppose your buyer was Eastside
Properties?"

"Why yes, how did you know?"

"Just a lucky guess. Thank you both. You've been
very helpful. I wish you both the best."

The Greens had confirmed everything we had suspected. Somehow, Riverside Realty was knee deep in whatever was going on in the neighborhood.

I moved back into the crowd and as I stood there marveling at the constant patter of the auctioneer, I felt something soft give me a nudge in my tushy. My first thought was that Maggie had tired of all this and what I had felt was an invitation to head for home and other less public activities.

I looked, and to my disappointment, I discovered it was the golden retriever's nose up my butt.

Not nearly as exciting.

I gave him a pat on the head, and off he went in search of other crotches to sniff.

I looked around the crowd and spotted Stan, an old acquaintance from my real estate days.

"Hi, Stan!" I shouted and raised my arm to give him a wave.

"Sold," bellowed the auctioneer. "To number 666, for $48!"

Oh crap! What did I do?

I burrowed my way through the crowd to try to undo my sale, but the auctioneer was three items down the road by the time I got there.

"Fine old table you got there, son," said an old gent in a cowboy hat.

Lucky me.

I looked at my purchase. It was an oak table about thirty inches square with ornate carved legs that ended with brass claws clutching inch-size round glass marbles.

It looked like a vulture had swooped down and plucked some unsuspecting guy's balls right out from under his winkie.

Maggie would be thrilled.

The sale ended, and we had bought the table from hell, a quilt, and a box of doilies.

After most of the cars and trucks had gone, I pulled my car up into the driveway and popped my trunk. I had carried the table about halfway across the yard when squish—I stepped in something soft and mushy. My timing was perfect. The big golden retriever had just dumped a load of hot dogs and funnel cakes, and I had found them. He gave my soiled foot a sniff and trotted off.

The mark of the beast!

CHAPTER 6

So far, a hooker who had been warned to leave our target area had been killed, a warehouse that a stubborn owner refused to sell had been torched and poor Spats Johnson's life had ended because he wouldn't part with The Blue Room.

Individual homeowners were between a rock and a hard place. Home values were plummeting as more and more sold homes were being boarded up, and the remaining sellers were grasping at straws trying to get what they could before it was too late. What businesses were left in the target area were on Troost.

One of the holdouts was the Cozy Corner, a gay bar. Like other businesses and homeowners, the proprietors of the Cozy Corner had been approached by Riverfront Realty with an offer to buy, but they refused. Threatening notes had been left, and the owners had come to the department for assistance.

Captain Short called the task force together to formulate a plan.

"Gentlemen, the owners and patrons of the Cozy Corner bar are being threatened. We're sure it's tied to the other illegal activity in the area, and we've got to get on top of it before we have another murder or fire. The perps won't come forward with uniformed officers on site, so we are going to an undercover operation, and we need two volunteers."

No one spoke or moved a muscle.

"Why thank you, Walt and Vince. I appreciate you stepping forward."

A round of applause, hoots, and hollers went up from the assembled officers.

Oh no, not again!

A couple of months ago I had been 'volunteered' as an undercover john at a strip club because I looked old and needy.

Now this!

I looked at Vince, and he just shook his head in disgust.

"Okay, why us?" I asked.

"Well, first of all you're old, and old guys aren't as threatening as young studs. Second, I think you and Vince make the perfect couple."

Another round of hoots and hollers.

Vince, a retired athletics coach, is sixty-five and a robust 175 pounds. I weigh 145 pounds soaking wet.

I have a head of gray hair, and Vince is probably gray too, but he shaves his head, so who knows?

Dooley, a young cop with a sense of humor, spoke up. "Well, I guess we know who's the 'he' and who's the 'she.'"

Another round of laughter.

If this continues I'm going to start developing self-image issues.

"We want you two to patronize the Cozy Corner for the next few nights and watch for any suspicious activity. If bar customers and employees are being threatened, we need to get a handle on it. Do you think you two can pull this off?"

"Gosh, I don't know," I said, looking at Vince. "I'm more into guys with hair."

"Don't let this fool you," Vince replied, rubbing his head. "It's really a solar panel for a sex machine."

I was willing to bet that he'd used that line before.

As the meeting broke up, one of the officers yelled, "Hey, Walt. Did you hear about the new gay sitcom? Leave it. It's Beaver!"

This was going to get really old, really fast.

That evening Vince and I sat in our car outside the Cozy Corner. Ox was patrolling the area in the black and white in case we needed backup.

"You ever been in one of these places?" I asked.

"Nope. You?"

"Nope. The only time I have ever been around the gay community was when I sold an apartment building whose tenants were all gay. It was probably the cleanest rental property I've ever seen. But there were some really strange pictures on the wall."

"How are we going to play this?" Vince asked. "I really like you, Walt, but I have my limits."

"Back at you. How about this is our first date and we don't know each other very well? That way we don't have to be too 'friendly.'"

"Sounds good to me. I just hope you're a fun date."

We entered the Cozy Corner and looked around. It looked just like any other bar in town except all of the couples were the same sex. The room was filled with soft music and muted conversations, and we got some long stares as we moved across the room.

New guys.

We took an empty table, and soon a young server approached.

"Haven't seen you in here before," he said. "What would you like to drink?"

"Margarita on the rocks for me," I said. I doubted they had Arbor Mist.

"Jack and Coke, please," Vince replied.

So far, so good.

Our drinks arrived, and we sat and sipped. We noticed that most of the other couples were huddled close together, some holding hands, some with arms entwined.

"What do you think?" I said. "Should we go for it? We don't want to look too frigid."

"What the hell," he said, and he stuck out his hands.

I really love holding hands with Maggie. They're so soft and dainty. I took Vince's hand in mine, and it felt like a handful of sausages.

I could tell Vince wasn't any more thrilled than I was.

It's just a job. It's just a job, I kept telling myself.

We were trying not to look too disgusted when two middle-aged guys walked over to our table.

"Hi, I'm Mike, and this is Larry. Do you mind if we join you?"

Well yeah, I mind, but it's just a job. Right?

"No, please have a seat. I'm Walt, and this is Vince."

Everyone shook hands.

"Larry and I are regulars here. Is this your first visit?"

"Actually, this is our first date," Vince said. "We haven't known each other that long."

"Well, congratulations! How did you two meet?"

Oops! We hadn't covered that.

I remembered an episode of *Two and a Half Men* where Alan and Charlie went to a gay party as partners. That was the first question they were asked. Where did you meet?

"Uh ... uh, we're both retired, and we both had part-time jobs at BuyMart. We met there."

That wasn't exactly a lie. We both worked there undercover for a week.

"I'm an attorney," Mike said. "And Larry's a stock broker. What did you guys do before you retired?"

"I was a realtor for thirty years," I replied.

I thought I'd let Vince make up his own occupation. I didn't know how well a gay guy spending forty years in a high school locker room would sound.

"I was a chef, uh, in Chicago, before I retired," Vince said.

Where did he come up with that?

About that time a smooth Michael Buble song filled the room, and I saw couples heading for the dance floor.

"Oh, I love that song," Larry said. "Come on, guys. Let's dance." They headed for the dance floor hand in hand.

"Do you know how to dance?" I asked.

"Not really."

"Well then, just follow my lead."

"How come you get to lead?"

"Because Maggie and I are ballroom dancers and I know what I'm doing."

"But I'm supposed to be the guy."

"Yeah, but you're going to look like a stupid guy if you don't know what you're doing. Look around. The 'guy' guy isn't always the one leading."

We made our way to the dance floor. I placed my arm around Vince's waist, and he placed his hand on my shoulder. He's three inches taller than me and thirty pounds heavier. I could only imagine how we looked.

"Okay," I said. "I'm going to lead with my left foot. You follow with your right foot."

"Gotcha."

I took a step forward and landed right on Vince's instep.

"Ow!"

I could tell that Vince was no Fred Astaire.

"Tell you what. Let's just rock from side to side. I'll step to my left, and you step to your right."

"Gotcha."

I stepped left and so did Vince. "No, your other right."

"Sorry."

"You were a football coach, right?

"Yep."

"Pretend you're a middle linebacker and the ball carrier is running off left tackle. Head for the running back and we'll be good. Then pretend on the next play he's running off right tackle."

"Gotcha."

We began to sway from side to side.

You just have to know how to communicate.

In a moment of clumsiness, Vince's cheek rubbed against mine.

"Good Lord, Vince, your face feels like fifty-grit sandpaper. If you're going to date me, you're going to have to shave closer than that."

"Well, your face isn't exactly as smooth as a baby's butt either."

Our first lovers' quarrel.

The rest of the evening proceeded without incident, and about midnight, we called it quits.

We met Ox on the street to compare notes. His night had been quiet too.

As we parted ways, Ox quipped, "I'm devastated, you know. I had no idea my partner was a two-timer."

Everyone's a comedian.

Since I didn't get home until one in the morning, I slept late.

I arose about 10:00 a.m., made a pot of coffee, and ate a bowl of Wheaties, 'The Breakfast of Champions.' At sixty-six, you need all the positive reinforcement you can get.

I dressed and headed downstairs to retrieve my morning newspaper. As soon as I stepped into the hall, I heard, "Hey, Walt, a horse walks into a bar, and the bartender says, 'Hey, buddy, why the long face?'"

"Jerry! I thought you were going to keep the jokes confined to the comedy club."

"Well, yeah, I know I promised, but I need to run my material by somebody before I put it on stage."

I thought for a moment. "Grab your jacket. We're going for a ride."

We got in the car and headed to my other building, the Three Trails Hotel.

We pulled up in front of the hotel, and I said to Jerry, "Here you go. A whole building full of retired guys looking for something to do. Entertain them to your heart's content."

"Really? And I won't get in trouble?"

"Not from me."

We headed up the front steps, and two of the retired residents, Mr. Feeney from number fourteen and Mr. Barnes from number sixteen were sitting on the swing. As we approached, we heard their conversation.

"Hey, Feeney. Look here. I just got a new hearing aid. It cost the VA four thousand dollars, but it's state of the art. It works perfect."

"Really?" Feeney replied. "What kind is it?"

"Twelve thirty."

Feeney thought for a minute then said "Windy, isn't it?"

"No," Barnes replied. "It's Thursday."

"So am I," Feeney said. "Let's go get a beer."

They walked off to Slick's Tavern.

"Wow! This is going to be a tough crowd," Jerry said.

Just then the front door flew open, and Mary bustled out.

"Morning, Walt. Don't be bringing me any new guys. We're all rented up."

"Hi, Mary. This is Jerry. He's already a tenant in my Armour building. He's in Milton's old place."

"Good to meet you," Mary said and stuck out her hand.

Mary is five feet, ten inches tall and weighs a hefty two hundred pounds. Jerry is five feet, four inches tall and weighs 125 pounds.

As they stood facing one another, Jerry's eyes and Mary's massive boobs were mere inches apart.

His stare lingered just a bit too long to suit Mary.

"Hey, buddy, I'm up here," she said, pointing to her eyes.

Jerry recovered quickly. "You know why guys have trouble making eye contact, don't you?"

"No. Why?"

"Because breasts don't have eyes."

Oh boy! We're in trouble now.

Mary just stood there a minute trying to make some sense of this weird conversation, and I was standing by, ready to pull Jerry out of harm's way, when Mary busted out laughing.

"I like this little guy," she said. She grabbed his head in her hands and stuffed his face in her ample cleavage.

"Holy cow, Mary! You're going to suffocate him!"

Finally Jerry pulled away and with a big grin said, "Good to meet your two."

You've got to admit he's quick.

The next afternoon at squad meeting, we got a ration of hoots and jabs from the guys.

They named us "the Gay Grandpas."

"Hey, Walt! Are you and Vince going steady yet?" Cop humor.

Unfortunately, we had nothing to report. The evening had unfolded without incident.

Well, except for my razor burn from Vince's whiskers.

Ox reported that all had been quiet on the streets around the Cozy Corner.

We decided to go back for another evening, and as the meeting broke up, wiseass Dooley shouted, "Hey, Walt, do you know how to tell if it's a gay western? All the good guys are hung!"

And I came out of retirement for this?

82

We arrived at the bar around nine, and Larry and Mike were already there.

"Hi, guys," they shouted across the floor. I guess they had adopted us.

We chatted and danced and drank and then chatted some more. Vince had picked up a few steps, so the dancing was not quite as painful as the night before.

We found out that Mike was a corporate attorney for a large firm and that Larry was struggling since the stock market had tanked.

Typical couples talk.

The evening passed without incident, and we left around 1:00 a.m.

The club and its patrons had been harassed before we started our undercover operation, and now we had spent two evenings there without incident.

It was almost nine thirty when I awoke the next morning. I was just not used to this wee-hours-of-the-morning stuff. I was usually in bed by 10:00 p.m. and considered it a victory if I made it through the news. This undercover stuff was totally wrecking my sleep cycle.

I brewed a pot of coffee, poured a cup, and headed to the front porch to get my morning paper.

It was early November, and I had bundled up in my robe anticipating a blast of early autumn chill.

Unlike James Whitcomb Riley, I wasn't excited about getting frost on my pumpkins. But as I stepped onto the porch, I was greeted by one of those special days that the good Lord gives us every once in a while just to remind us that He's still up there.

The sun was shining, and a warm breeze more like May than November sent fallen leaves scurrying across the lawn. This was a day to savor.

Apparently I wasn't the only soul enjoying the autumn splendor.

Bernice Crenshaw, my sweet little eighty-three-year-old from 2-B, was on one side of the porch talking with Henrietta Krug from down the block, and my eighty-five-year-old professor from UMKC, Leopold Skinner from 2-A, was conversing with her husband, Homer Krug.

I bid them all good morning, retrieved my paper, and sat on the front step with my coffee.

I started to read the headlines but was soon thoroughly distracted by their most intriguing conversation.

"How you been feeling lately?" Bernice asked.

"Not too bad, all things considered," she replied.

"You ever heard the Reverend Billy Bob Parsons on TV?"

"Can't say as I have."

"Well, you really ought to watch him. Homer and I were watching the other night, and I was having a real bad pain in my stomach. The Reverend Billy Bob said that if I was to put one hand on my side and my other hand on the TV, I would be healed.

"But just as I was about to do it, Homer jumped up and put one hand on his crotch and the other on the TV. I told him, 'Sit down, Homer; this is for the healing of the sick, not the raising of the dead.'"

I guess Henrietta just didn't believe in miracles.

Then, from the other side of the porch, Homer was getting in his licks.

"Professor," Homer said, "Henrietta and I just celebrated our fiftieth wedding anniversary."

"Congratulations, Homer. Did you do anything special?"

"I'll say we did. As we were sitting at the breakfast table, I said to Henrietta, 'Fifty years ago today we were sitting together like this completely nekkid.' She grinned at me and said, 'You want to do it again?' So we did.

"We went to the bedroom and stripped buck nekkid, and when we got back to the table, she said to me, 'Homer, my nipples are just as hot for you today as they were fifty years ago.'"

"'Well, of course they are,' I told her. 'One of them is in your coffee, and the other is in your oatmeal.'"

Not exactly like the stories I used to hear in the locker room.

One of the professor's traits is to lace his conversation with words of wisdom from some old master, and after listening to this graphic account of Homer's love life, he simply said, "The bonds of matrimony are a good investment if the interest is kept up."

Sounds like the Krugs are still collecting interest after fifty years.

Bernice and the professor grew weary after a while and went back to their apartments, and the Krugs drifted back down the street. I was finally alone on the porch. While I enjoy the company of my neighbors, I was anxious to sip my coffee and read my morning paper in peace and revel in the glorious morning.

Just as I was settling in, the door flew open, and out came Willie and Jerry.

So much for solitude.

"Hey, Mr. Walt, how's it hanging?"

Knowing Willie, I recognized this as street version of "Good morning, Walt. How are you today?"

With my weird schedule the past few days, I hadn't had the opportunity to visit with either of my colorful neighbors.

Willie had been uncharacteristically quiet and withdrawn since the murder and funeral of his friend, Doris. Instead of his boyish exuberance, he seemed introspective and deep in thought. I took his cocky salutation as a sign that the old Willie was back.

"Anything cookin' wit de investigation?"

I hadn't told Willie about our undercover operation, so I shared my story about Vince and me at the Cozy Corner gay bar.

Naturally, I had expected to get a ration of hoots and hollers, and I wasn't disappointed.

"Ooh, you and Vince doin' de 'swishy' thing. I wish I could see dat! I been thinkin' about redecoratin' my apartment. Maybe you guys could give me some help."

Stereotypes.

Of course Jerry had to add his two cents' worth. "Walt, I know I promised to lay off the jokes, but I've got a good one maybe you could share with your gay buddies."

"Swell. Let's hear it."

"Two gay guys are standing on a bridge watching ships pass by underneath them. One says to the other, 'What kind of ship is that?'

"'Container.'

"'Okay, what's that one over there?'

"'Oil tanker.'

"'How about that one?'

"'That's a ferry boat.'

"'Really? I knew we were strong, but I never knew we had our own navy!'"

Yeah, I'm sure I'll share that with the guys tonight.

Then Willie grew serious. "Mr. Walt, you gotta be really careful. Dere's some bad stuff goin' down in dat neighborhood. I been keepin' in touch wit Louie de Lip since Doris got whacked. He don't even go der no mo'."

"Thanks, Willie. I'll be careful. We've been there two nights, and it's been really quiet."

"Yeah, well maybe it's jus' de quiet befo' de storm."

About 9:00 p.m., Vince and I left the station and headed to the Cozy Corner for our third date.

The bar was never loud or boisterous, just couples enjoying each other's company insulated from the rude and judgmental forces outside those walls.

But this night something was different.

Instead of the dozen or more couples we had seen on previous nights, there were just two guys in one booth in the back of the room.

"Hey, Stevie, where is everybody tonight?"

The bartender motioned us over and spoke in a low whisper, "I guess you guys haven't heard."

"Heard what?"

"About Mike and Larry. They left the bar about twenty minutes after you last night, and someone jumped them on the way to their car, beat the crap out of them, and left a note saying, 'You faggots keep coming here, you'll be maggot food.'"

"Are they okay?"

"They're both in the hospital with bruises, contusions, and some cracked ribs, but they'll live. Everyone's scared to death. That's why no one's here tonight. If this keeps up, we'll have to shut the place down."

We ordered drinks and went to our table.

"Well, whoever is behind all this is getting just what they want," Vince murmured. "A boarded-up bar in this neighborhood won't be worth spit. I'll bet Eastside Properties will be right there to buy it for a song."

"I feel terrible about Mike and Larry," I replied. "They were great guys. We had better let the captain know what's going on. Whoever took the report may have just chalked it up to another mugging, not realizing this was connected to our investigation."

I reached for my cell phone.

"Oh crap! I left my phone in the car. Where's yours?"

Vince felt his pockets. "Guess I didn't bring mine at all. I left home in kind of a hurry."

"Great pair of cops we are," I said. "Order me another margarita. I'll be right back."

I headed to the car.

The bar is situated on a corner lot facing Troost Avenue. You can park on the street, but we parked in the bars lighted off street parking lot in back, which enters off the side street.

The lot was well lit when we arrived, but as I headed for our car, I noticed the floods were out.

Must've burnt out a bulb, I thought. *I gotta remember to tell Stevie.*

I had just hit the remote button to unlock the car door when a shadowy figure leaped from behind a car and planted a meaty fist in my belly. I doubled over in pain, and as I desperately tried sucking air into my lungs, a canvas bag was thrown over my head.

"I guess you faggots just can't take a hint. When they find your body tomorrow, they'll know we mean business."

I had sucked in enough air to at least stand upright again, and I started searching my feeble old mind trying to remember some of the hand-to-hand techniques the PT instructor had shared with us a few months ago.

I needn't have bothered. The last thing I remember was a sharp whack, a blinding pain in my skull, and everything going black.

When consciousness returned, I found myself in the trunk of a car.

My hands were tied behind my back, and my head hurt like hell. At least he had taken the bag off my head, but it didn't really matter. The trunk was pitch black.

I had no idea how long I had been out, so I had no idea how far we had traveled. We could be anywhere.

Had Vince missed me yet? Had he called for backup? Were my fellow officers trying to find me? Would I soon be dead?

Dead!

It's amazing what pops into your mind when you think the next few minutes might be your last.

I had just been kidnapped! Of all the things that I could have thought about, the first stupid thing that came to mind was a Rodney Dangerfield quip: "I remember the time I was kidnapped and they sent a piece of my finger to my father. He said he wanted more proof!"

The human mind is a strange thing.

Then I thought about Maggie. Would I ever see her again? Did she really know how I felt about her? How would this affect her life?

I read once that if you want to know how important you are, stick your finger in a bucket of water, pull it out, and see what's left behind. That's a pretty pessimistic attitude.

I thought about Maggie and Willie and Mary and the professor and all of the people who were part of my life, and somehow I just didn't believe I wouldn't be missed.

Then it occurred to me that I wasn't dead yet.

I remembered a quote from Tarzan out of one of my comic books I read as a kid: "Where there is life, there is hope."

I need a plan, I thought, *but I don't even know who's got me, not to mention where we are.*

Just then I felt the car slow down, turn a corner, and come to a stop.

I was about to find out.

The lid popped open, and I was staring into the face of Joey Piccolo.

He grabbed me by the arms and rolled me out of the trunk. Without the use of my hands, I landed with an unceremonious thump.

"On your feet, faggot," he snarled and gave me a kick in the ribs.

I struggled to my feet, looked around, and recognized where he had taken me.

The west side of Kansas City sits on a hill overlooking the West Bottoms and the Missouri River. Quality Hill is just a few blocks east.

This location is noted for the beautiful panoramic view of the valley lying several hundred feet below. The street ends in a park-like setting with a walking path and a low concrete wall separating the path from the sheer drop into the valley. Small covered viewing areas are located right on the edge of the precipice.

Maggie and I have stopped by here on occasion to enjoy the view and sometimes neck like a couple of teenagers.

The cliff is visited often during daylight hours but seldom at night. It's just one of those places you know are off limits after dark.

This night, of course, no one else was around. I suspected that Joey and his goons were the reason sane people didn't go there.

He pushed me roughly in the direction of the wall where the drop was the steepest.

I saw the .38 in his hand, and I remembered how Doris, the homeless guy and Spats had met their fate. They say bad things come in threes.

We reached the wall, and he kicked the back of my legs, bringing me to my knees.

I remembered seeing photos in *Life* magazine of prisoners of war being executed by their captors, and I remembered the horror I had felt.

I wondered how human beings could do things like that to each other.

Here I was and I still didn't understand.

I knelt there with my head bowed and felt the cold steel press against the back of my head. I held my breath waiting for the end.

Out of the darkness, a dark figure sprinted in our direction. The utter quiet of the moment was shattered by a piercing scream.

Joey was even more surprised than I was, and as he pulled the gun from the back of my head and turned it toward his attacker, the black blur hit him squarely in the chest.

The gun flew from his hand, and he stumbled backwards, his momentum carrying him to the retaining wall and over the edge. We heard his last pitiful wail that ended abruptly as he hit the valley floor below.

I got to my feet and looked for the hero who had saved my life, and there, picking himself up after his smashing tackle, was my old friend Willie.

He rushed to my side and cut my bonds with his pocket knife.

"You okay, Mr. Walt?"

I couldn't speak. I just grabbed him and held him close.

When I finally regained my senses, I asked, "Willie, what in the world are you doing here?"

"Afta wot happen to Doris, I knew you was playin' with some mean dudes. Dat asshole done took someone special from me, and I'll be damned if I was gonna let him take you too. I been keepin' an eye on you and Vince, but I didn't say nothin' cause I knew you'd tell me no. I saw Joey take you tonight, and Louie de Lip and I followed. Got here jus' in time, I guess."

People often hear about the guys that land planes in rivers and save children from burning buildings and brand them heroes, and they are, of course.

Few people will ever know that Willie Duncan is a hero, but to me, he's the greatest hero of all.

CHAPTER 7

It was nearly dawn by the time the detectives and CSI guys finished processing the crime scene.

The EMT checked me out, and with the exception of the goose egg on my head and sore ribs, I was pronounced physically fit.

Emotionally, not so much.

When I didn't return to the bar right away, Vince had gone looking for me. Finding the parking lot empty, he summoned Ox, and they called for backup. They, of course, had no idea where to start looking.

Imagine their surprise when my whereabouts was phoned in by Louie the Lip. Due to his notorious reputation, Louie wasn't exactly on the cops' citizen of the year list. After the officers sorted out the details of my rescue and Louie's contribution was noted, I think he may have earned himself a get-out-of-jail-free card for his next offense.

Naturally, Willie was the man of the hour. Vince and Ox couldn't thank him enough for saving my sorry ass, but Willie wanted no part of the spotlight. He had spent his life staying just below the radar, and the last thing he wanted was some hotshot reporter digging into his past for a story. His only public comment was, "I jus' glad Mr. Walt is okay an' dat scumbag got what was comin' to him."

After the detectives had taken their statements, Willie and Louie disappeared into the night.

Later, ballistics matched the .38 that had been recovered at the scene to the three previous murders. We now knew who had killed Doris, the homeless man and Spats, but were no closer to knowing why.

It was 6:00 a.m. when Ox dropped me off at my apartment. I was exhausted, an emotional wreck, and I hurt like hell. I took two Tylenol and fell into bed.

The next thing I heard was a loud and persistent banging on my front door. I tried to ignore it, hoping whomever it was would give up and go away.

No such luck.

The pounding became more insistent, and from the hallway I heard, "Open this door, you jerk!"

Oh my God! Maggie!

My condition, being as it was, had caused me to make a grievous error in judgment. I hadn't called her.

I slid the bolt on the door, and the fiery little red-head burst into my apartment and grabbed me by the shirt.

"You jerk!" she screamed, her piercing green eyes boring into mine. "I had to hear about my lover being kidnapped by a murderer on the news! How could you do that to me?"

What could I say? I just stood there looking stupid and hurt.

I had prepared myself for another volley when a tear replaced the fire in her eye. Then I heard a sob and felt her body shudder as she pulled me close to her. "I don't know what I'd do if something happened to you," she wailed. "I love you so much."

Then, just as quickly, the fire returned. "If you ever do that to me again, you won't have to worry about a hit man. I'll take you out myself."

"Yes, ma'am. I understand."

Then Maggie's nurturing instinct took over. She held me, coddled me, and fed me, and finally we tumbled into bed.

We lay there and talked for hours. Okay, maybe it wasn't all talk.

The captain had insisted that I take a few days off to heal and get my head back in the game. Maggie had appointments scheduled, which she offered to cancel, but I assured her I was fine, and reluctantly she left.

But I wasn't fine.

In my few short months on the force, I had been shot at by a gangbanger and a crazy real estate agent, beaten by a Latino thug, and now nearly executed by a mob hit man.

There's something about a near-death experience that shakes you to the core and makes you keenly aware of your mortality.

I had been rolling the dice and winning, but for how long? If you keep rolling, you're bound to 'crap out' sometime. Only in this game, the stakes are your life.

Something told me it was time to pay a visit to my old pal Pastor Bob.

While I have never doubted the existence of a higher power, I must admit I haven't spent that much time at Sunday morning services.

Growing up, my mother insisted I attend Sunday school at the local Methodist church. My dad, though not agnostic or atheist, was at the very least indifferent, and when Mom passed away, so did my incentive to attend church.

I took a comparative religions class in college and went away even more confused. My grandma used to say, "There's more than one way to skin a cat," so I guess I can understand why there are so many different paths that hopefully lead us to the same end. The thing I don't understand is why people fight about it.

Throughout recorded history, wars have been fought, atrocities have been committed, and millions have died in the name of organized religion.

It's still happening today.

Sometimes it seems our churches are more about politics than worship.

That's how I came to know Pastor Bob.

He was the pastor at a large Protestant congregation numbering several thousand, and his parishioners loved him. But his church, along with so many of our cherished institutions, was subverted by the influence of big business, and he felt increasing pressure from the church hierarchy to expound their political views from the pulpit. He refused to give in to the pressure and was issued an ultimatum: get in line or get out.

His message to the church board was a passage from the twenty-second chapter of Matthew, "Render therefore unto Caesar the things that are Caesar's; and unto God the things that are God's."

And he walked away.

Not surprisingly, many in the congregation walked away with him.

I was on duty at the real estate office when Pastor Bob walked in and said he needed a church building—cheap.

The turbulent sixties were a distant memory, and Midtown Kansas City was in the midst of a cultural transformation as minority families relocated into previously all-white neighborhoods. 'White flight' had become a buzzword, and as longtime residents pulled up stakes and moved south, churches they had previously attended boarded up their doors. I found a board-up on Linwood Boulevard, just a few blocks from my Three Trails Hotel that fit the bill.

In less than a year, Pastor Bob and his nondenominational flock had remodeled the building and found a permanent home.

I really liked Pastor Bob, and we became close friends.

His philosophy of life and mine seemed in tune. Plus, he has a great sense of humor. Whenever his flock gets too uptight, he loves to use the John Wesley quote, "Sour godliness is the devil's religion."

You know a guy is okay if he has a church bowling league who call themselves the 'Holy Rollers.'

We often go to Mel's Diner and discuss life and theology over a plate of biscuits and gravy.

Once, I was feeling some guilt about my lack of church attendance and wondered whether my soul was in mortal danger. I'll always remember his reply: "Going to church doesn't make you a Christian any more than standing in a garage makes you a car."

In a more somber moment, as we discussed what makes us do what we do, I said, "I've always tried to live my life so as not to hurt the ones I love and to treat other people like I want to be treated."

He just smiled and said, "You know, I think I've read that somewhere before. Oh yeah, I remember. I think it was in the first four chapters of the New Testament."

One Sunday after Jerry the Joker moved into my building, we went together to a morning service.

Pastor Bob's sermon touched on remorse. "Many people sow wild oats on a Saturday night then come to church on Sunday praying for a crop failure."

Jerry burst out laughing, which I don't think was the reaction Pastor Bob was looking for.

On the way out, as we shook hands, Jerry asked if he could use the line in his comedy club routine.

But he couldn't stop there. "Oh, by the way, do you know what Winnie the Pooh and John the Baptist have in common? Their middle name."

You gotta love it.

I found Pastor Bob in his study.

He had a genuine look of concern when I walked in. "Good Lord, Walt. Are you all right? I heard what happened on the news."

"I've been better, but I guess I'll live. At least I hope I will. That's what I came to talk to you about."

"Let's hear it."

I shared with him all my narrow escapes and near-death experiences. "Am I stupid to keep doing this? Am I tempting fate?"

"What is your definition of fate, Walt? Do you believe some higher power has given you a finite number of close calls and you've used them all up?"

"Well, now that you've put it in those terms, not really."

"Why did you start doing what you're doing now? What possessed you to become a cop?"

"This may sound a bit melodramatic, but I just had a sense that there was a lot of injustice in the world and that maybe I could make a difference."

"And have you?"

I thought about what Ox and Vince and Willie and Mary and I had accomplished in the last year. "Yeah, I think maybe we have."

"So what's changed? You all done cleaning up the streets? No more bad guys to catch? Or maybe you figure you've caught your share and now it's somebody else's turn?"

Whoa, back off, I thought.

"You've been close enough to death to taste it. Are you afraid to die?"

See, this is why I don't talk to preachers. They make you think about stuff you don't want to face.

"If you came in here wanting me to tell you to back off, I can't do it. There are few things in life I know for certain, but one of them is that God has given us the ability to make decisions on our own. It's called free will. You have to look into your heart, and if you feel like you're through, then quit. But if you feel like you have more to give, it's your decision to keep going."

Okay, Bob, why don't you tell me what you really think?

"And furthermore, if you decide to keep going, don't expect me to give you a St. Benedict medal to hang around your neck and promise that you'll be okay. You could decide to quit and get hit by a car going home, or the next guy you apprehend could stick a knife in your ribs, or you could live to a ripe old age and die quietly in your sleep."

"So what's your point?"

"My point is that we can't know the future. We can only live our lives and make our decisions following the dictates of our heart. Another thing I know for certain is that we're all going to die sooner or later, and to paraphrase Shakespeare's Julius Caesar, 'A coward dies a thousand deaths: a brave man dies but once.'"

"Deep stuff. I guess that's why they pay you preachers the big bucks."

"Walt, has anyone ever told you that you are a jerk?"

"Yeah, Maggie told me that yesterday. It must be true. Two of my favorite people can't be wrong."

"You look kind of washed out; what did you have for breakfast this morning?"

"Just a cup of coffee and all that bull you just forced down my throat."

"I'm going to takes off my preacher's hat and put on my good buddy hat for my next piece of advice."

"Okay, lay it on me."

"How about we go to Mel's for a platter of biscuits and gravy?"

Now there's some advice that's easy to swallow.

CHAPTER 8

After stuffing myself with Mel's biscuits and white cream gravy, I headed home hoping to just enjoy some peace and quiet and reflect on Pastor Bob's words of wisdom.

I had just settled into my easy chair when I heard a knock on the door.

So much for peace and quiet.

I opened the door, and an agitated Willie burst in. "Mr. Walt, I hope you ain't doing nuthin' 'cause I needs a favor."

"And what exactly would that be?"

"Do you remember my fren' Brother Hank, de preacher at de Mt. Zion Community Church?"

"Sure, I remember Brother Hank. He preached at Doris's funeral service."

"Yeah, dat's him. Well, Spats, the guy what got hisself whacked at the Blue Room was Brother Hank's pappy."

"Really?" I hadn't made the connection.

"Sho nuff, and when he was goin' through ole Spats's stuff, dey foun' somethin' I think you gonna want to hear."

"What? Jazz? Blues? Benny Burton, told us that Spats was quite a musician."

"Dat's fo' sure. He was one of de best sax players dis town ever seen. Back in de day, he played wit some of de greatest jazz musicians der ever was. His daddy was Pete Johnson, who played jazz piano wif Count Basie, Joe Turner, and Hot Lips Page.

"But his hero and mentor was Charlie 'Yardbird' Parker. Spats heard Ole Pete an' de Bird playin' in de late 1930s in joints like De Chocolate Bar, Dante's Inferno, and de Pla-Mor Ballroom."

"Okay, sounds interesting, but what am I going to be listening to?"

"I ain't tellin' 'cause I don't want to spoil it, but I know you gonna want to hear it."

So, reluctantly, I left the comfort of my easy chair, dressed, and we were off to see the Reverend Henry Johnson, or Brother Hank as he preferred to be called.

On the way over, I called Pastor Bob for some background information.

"Sure, I know Brother Hank. We work together on the Mid-City Ecumenical Council. That's a group of pastors from all denominations who focus primarily on ministry to the inner city. The Salvation Army and City Union Mission do great work there, but there is just so much need that the churches pitch in and do what they can. We have a homeless shelter and a refuge for battered women. Hank's a great guy."

I thanked him and signed off just as we were pulling into the church lot.

Brother Hank and his wife, Gracie, met us at the door. After introductions, he led us to his pastor's study.

"Thank you so much for coming. We didn't know who to talk to about this, and when Willie shared your background with us, we hoped you might help."

"Well, you certainly have my attention. What can I do for you?"

"In order for this to make any sense at all, I need to give you some background information.

"During the 1930s, Kansas City was a wide-open swinging town. These were the prohibition years, and while the rest of the country was dry, booze flowed freely in K.C. under the leadership of political boss Tom Pendergast. In fact, Kansas City became known as 'The Paris of the Plains.' Jazz clubs, speakeasies, and brothels flourished. At one time there were over fifty clubs on Twelfth Street alone.

"It was during this time that my grandfather, Pete Johnson, played with greats like Charlie Parker. My dad, Orville 'Spats' Johnson, was just a kid, but he grew up listening to all the jazz greats and became a fantastic musician in his own right.

"In 1940, Pendergast was arrested for tax evasion, and that brought an end to Kansas City's golden age of jazz. Kansas City jazz continued to be world famous, but on a much smaller scale.

"Dad played in The Blue Room until the day he was murdered. After we laid Pappy to rest, we started going through his things. He was eighty years old and his whole life was music, so you can imagine how much stuff he had collected. Stuff like this."

On the desk was an old reel-to-reel tape recorder. I hadn't seen one in years.

"We found everything from old 78 RPM records to show bills from the jazz clubs of the 30s. There was a recording studio in the back of one of the clubs, and the guys would get together and jam almost every day. There were dozens of these old reels, and we had planned on boxing them up and donating them to the American Jazz Museum over on Vine. We decided to take a break, and we threw a few of the old reels on the recorder while we rested.

"Then we heard this."

He flipped on the recorder, and I had expected to hear Louie Armstrong or Jonah Jones, but when I heard the first few bars of the old blues classic:

I went down.
Down to St. James Infirmary.
Saw my baby laying there.

It was the unmistakable voice of Elvis Presley.

I sat dumbfounded, listening to the King of Rock 'n' Roll's interpretation of *Mack The Knife*, *Lullaby of Birdland*, *My Blue Heaven*, and a dozen other blues standards.

I'm no music expert, but I do know Elvis.

Elvis was born in 1935, and I was born in 1943. In 1956, when the twenty-one-year-old rocker recorded *Heartbreak Hotel,* I was thirteen and owned a high-fidelity record player.

The first time I heard him, I was hooked.

The minute a Presley record was released, I was first in line at the Katz Drugstore record department. I bought all of the 45 RPM original releases, and I still have them, fifty-three years later.

My collection includes 45s, 33 RPM albums, cassettes, and CDs. I have all of his movies and concert appearances.

In my early years in real estate, I would buy old apartment buildings in need of repair, and with Elvis singing by my side, I rehabbed the heck out of them.

Elvis recorded hundreds of songs. He could sing anything from country to rock 'n' roll to gospel, and I'm pretty sure I have them all.

But I didn't have these.

Once I had my wits about me, I turned to Brother Hank.

"Who knows about these?"

"Just the people in this room."

I turned to Willie. "Have you told anyone else about this?"

"No, sir! Not a word."

"Good, let's keep it that way. If these are genuine, and I believe they are, they are worth millions."

"No shit?" Willie exclaimed. Then with a look of contrition, he said, "Oh, sorry, Brother Hank."

"Do you have a secure place you can lock these up until I can do some research?"

"We can keep them in the church safe."

"Great. Do it immediately, and don't breathe a word of this to anyone. Make no mistake; people would kill for these tapes."

I noticed that there were dates inscribed on the tape boxes, and I scribbled down the date on the Elvis boxes: June 18, 1977.

I was in a daze as I drove back to my apartment. The impact of this find was inconceivable.

Imagine finding another Rogers and Hammerstein's *South Pacific* or another rhapsody by George Gershwin. Those would pale in comparison to this discovery.

Elvis is just as popular today as when he was alive. Thousands of mourners flock to Graceland each year on the anniversary of his death, and there are birthday celebrations on January eighth all over the world. Elvis fans can't get enough of the King, and an album with new songs, never heard before, would rock the music world to its very foundation.

But where did it come from?

I warned Willie once again not to utter a word to anyone, and I began my search on the Internet and in the many books of Elvis's life in my collection.

I had an idea, but I needed confirmation.

Elvis had appeared in concert in Kansas City several times. I had seen him in person myself, but I couldn't quite pin down the date of his last appearance.

Then I found it.

The date of Elvis's last concert appearance in Kansas City was June 18, 1977, the exact date on Brother Hank's tape.

The article went on to say that Elvis's last concert appearance was a few days later on June 26, in Indianapolis, Indiana. Six weeks later, he was dead.

Having read extensively of Elvis's life and having seen many videos of his performances, I knew that often after a concert he was so wired that he couldn't sleep, so he would gather his fellow musicians and friends and jam until the wee hours of the morning.

He grew up in Memphis and loved the Beal Street Blues. Many of his early rockabilly hits were remakes of tunes that originated in the black nightclubs. His famous *Hound Dog* was a remake of the same song by Big Mama Thornton.

It wasn't a stretch to see Elvis leave Kemper Arena with his entourage and hook up with Spats Johnson and his band in the back room of a Kansas City jazz club.

A jazz club with a recording studio.

It's fascinating how sometimes real life can imitate art.

One of my favorite movies of all time is *Eddie and the Cruisers*. It's a story about a fictitious rock 'n' roll singer named Eddie Wilson. In his heyday, he mysteriously died when his '57 Chevy plunged off a bridge. The plot focused on Eddie's last recording session and the disappearance of the tapes after his death. In the end, when the tapes surfaced, it was, of course, a major event in music history.

Only this wasn't Eddie Wilson, it was Elvis Presley, who changed the course of music in America.

I got chills just thinking about it.

I knew a lot about music, but I knew nothing about the music business.

It was time to get some advice from an expert, so I called my friend Lee Dresser of The Krazy Kats.

He had been in the music business over fifty years and had played and rubbed shoulders with the likes of Dean Martin, Jimmie Rogers, Bo Diddly, Pat Boone, and Fats Domino, plus the Kats had their own albums and CDs.

I found Lee at home and without revealing specifics told him the story of the lost Elvis tapes.

I waited for a response but heard nothing but silence. "Lee, are you there?"

Finally, he spoke. "Walt, you have no idea what you have there or the can of worms this discovery will open. All the public ever sees is the final product when it hits the store shelves. The music business is a dog-eat-dog world run by huge corporations with limitless resources. My advice to your friend is this: hire the best attorney he can find who is an expert in copyright and business law because as soon as the word is out, there will be a dozen corporations claiming ownership of those tapes, from the Elvis Presley foundation to RCA Victor Records.

"If he isn't careful from the beginning, he could lose it all in a legal battle. Where are the tapes?"

"They're in a small home safe."

"They should be in a bank safety deposit box that only he knows about."

"Gosh, Lee, you make it sound like we've got the launch code to the U.S. missile system."

"What you have is probably worth more than that. When word gets out, the album will go platinum overnight before it's even released. Elvis may be dead, but his music certainly isn't. Last year, thirty-two years after his death, his estate earned over fifty-five million dollars. That's more that he made in a year when he was alive. People kill for that kind of money."

"Okay, so what should he do after he finds an attorney?"

"I assume your friend has no experience in the recording business, so once his attorney has protected the asset, he should start negotiations with a major recording company. The tapes have to be digitally remastered and an album produced."

"Any ideas where to start?"

"Yeah, I have a few. Let me get some names and numbers for you."

I thanked Lee and promised to keep him in the loop as things progressed.

I met with Brother Hank and Gracie and shared the information I had gleaned so far. I impressed on them the need for secrecy and diligence, not just for the tapes, but for their own safety as well.

They thanked me, took the list that Lee had provided, and promised they would proceed with utmost caution.

The music world was about to get the biggest jolt since the death of Michael Jackson.

CHAPTER 9

It was difficult to concentrate on work knowing what I knew.

I was busting to tell someone, but I couldn't even share the exciting news with Maggie. There was just too much at stake.

I checked in with Brother Hank every few days. He told me they had hired a very expensive lawyer and things were progressing, but very slowly.

Unfortunately, our investigation had stalled. The next two weeks were agonizingly slow as we went over the evidence time after time.

Our target area was from the freeway on the west to Paseo Avenue on the east and from Independence Avenue on the north to Truman Road on the south.

It was turning into a desolate wasteland. Dozens of homeowners had sold out to Eastside Properties via Riverfront Realty, and the only thing we could pin on anyone was a possible blockbusting violation by Riverfront if we could find a homeowner with enough guts to file a complaint.

All the homes purchased by Eastside sat boarded up and empty. All but a few of the remaining occupied homes were up for sale and like the other homes before them would remain on the market until the seller lowered his price to a giveaway level.

Most businesses had given up as the population dwindled, and several of the holdouts had mysteriously burned.

Even Cozy Corner had thrown in the towel. Word had spread that Joey Piccolo, who had been threatening the bar patrons, was dead, but knowing Joey's connection to the mob, everyone knew there would be another thug ready to move in and take his place.

We felt like Hercules fighting the Hydra. Every time he cut off one head, three grew in its place.

Street people had been warned away from the area, and corners where once hookers, pimps, and druggies conducted their business now stood empty.

And to make matters worse, every time we thought we had a lead, we came up empty. Joey had slipped through our fingers, and two drug busts tipped by usually reliable sources netted us nothing but vacant buildings. Nobody said it publicly, but everyone wondered if there was a leak in the department.

We knew that Joey Piccolo was responsible for three murders, but there was no physical evidence to tie any of them to the Lorenzo or Mancuso families.

Dead ends everywhere.

The days wore on, and our thoughts focused on the upcoming holiday, Thanksgiving.

For the past few years, Thanksgiving had been kind of hit and miss. Maggie and I were both immersed in real estate and didn't have the inclination to plan anything fancy, so we usually just wound up in a nice restaurant somewhere.

Bernice and the professor sometimes shared a meal, as did Willie and Mary. But this year was going to be different. Things had happened in each of our lives that seemed to draw us together, and there was a mutual feeling that we wanted to share the holiday.

It was decided that the event would take place in my apartment. Maggie and I would do the bird, and each guest would bring his or her favorite side dish or dessert.

What a plan.

We started counting noses: Maggie and I, Vince, Ox, the professor, Willie, Mary, Bernice, and Jerry, nine in all, a full house.

I have many fond memories of Thanksgivings past. My earliest recollections were at my grandparents' farm. Mom and Dad would bring a couple of side dishes, but the bulk of the meal was all Grandma. She could really cook.

The big bird always came out golden brown, tender, and juicy, and Irish potatoes were whipped to a snowy peak just waiting to be smothered in butter and rich, creamy gravy. Homemade yeast rolls as big as my fist held just the right amount of Grandma's strawberry jelly. Sweet potatoes were baked in butter, brown sugar, and white sugar, and a layer of jumbo marshmallows was added just before serving.

Mom usually brought a casserole of French cut green beans baked in mushroom gravy, topped with those crunchy little onion things.

And, of course, what would Thanksgiving be without pumpkin pie topped with real whipped cream.

I think I gained three pounds just thinking about it. As the big day drew near, I felt my excitement build.

I was anxious to share the day with my friends. I just knew it would be a huge success. How could it not be? After all, I learned watching the very best.

Maggie came over the night before so we could prepare the table and get an early start.

I love Maggie, and she has many sterling qualities. Cooking isn't one of them. She is, after all, a career woman. On the nights we eat at home, it's usually order in or bring home.

We're on a first-name basis with the Domino's delivery guy.

I'm pretty much in the same boat except for my tuna casserole.

We had purchased the turkey several days earlier. When we brought it home, it was frozen solid as a rock. I carefully read the directions on the shrink-wrap. "Place in refrigerator to thaw."

Okay, sounds right.

So the bird went in the fridge, and we just left it there.

See you in a couple of days.

That evening we scrounged extra card tables to accommodate our guests, butted them all up together, and discovered my only tablecloth was about two feet short of covering the top.

No problem; I remembered an old nursery rhyme, "Mary, Mary, will you get up. We need the sheets for the table." I figured if it were good enough for the Brothers Grimm or Mother Goose, it would probably work for us.

My only sheets were emblazoned with the image of Superman flying above Metropolis. I thought they were pretty cool when I bought them. He is, after all, one of my heroes.

After a quick wash and dry, we started to set the table, Superman and all. With strategic placement of the dishes and silver, probably no one would notice the extra guest.

Dishes!

I had lived alone for years. On the rare occasions I had guests, it was usually just one other person.

I don't have a dishwasher. I have a drain board with one of those wire thingys for your dishes to dry in. I eat, wash my plate and fork, and put it in the dryer thingy, and it's right there waiting for my next meal. I couldn't remember when they were actually put back in the cabinet or when their three companion pieces saw the light of day.

Yep, that's right. I own four place settings and we had nine people coming. What now?

I started making calls, and Willie came to my rescue. He said he had all the paper plates I would need, so I hotfooted it to the basement, and he handed me a stack of plates with clown faces. He said he had gotten a heck of a deal on them from the discount bin at Dollar General.

117

Peachy.

With the clown face plates gracing our table covered with a Superman sheet, the only word that came to mind was colorful.

Actually, another word came to mind, but since it was not in tune with the holiday spirit, I let it pass.

Our next stop was the fridge to check on our twenty-two-pound turkey. He was still there, of course, and frozen solid to the inside of the refrigerator wall.

Oh crap! I had followed the directions on the shrink-wrap. What happened? Then I noticed the setting on the thermostat: coldest, all the way over.

I pulled our arctic bird out of the fridge and clunked it on the counter. We both just stood and stared at the frigid fowl.

"Any suggestions?" I asked.

"Yeah, but you wouldn't like any of them."

Then it came to me. "No problem. Let's give our baby a bath."

I grabbed the bird, and we headed to the bathroom. I turned the hot water on all the way and filled the tub until it covered the turkey.

"This will thaw it out in no time," I said. "Let's go have a glass of Arbor Mist. It should be ready by the time we finish."

We polished off a round of wine and headed to the bathroom. The water was ice cold, and Mr. Bird was still stiff as a poker.

"Well, maybe another round will take care of it," I said as I drained and refilled the tub.

By this time it was 9:00 p.m., and I was exhausted. "We can't go to bed until that thing is thawed," Maggie sighed.

So we took turns, and every hour throughout the night, one of us was up bathing our turkey.

The next morning it dawned on me why God gives childrearing to the young. Thank you, Lord!

I stumbled into the kitchen. "It's 6:00 a.m. Coffee—I need coffee."

"I'll make the coffee. You go get the bird," Maggie muttered.

I went to the bathroom, and there he was, right where we left him. I figured if he still had one, he'd be laughing his ass off.

After a pot of coffee and a piece of toast, I began to feel better.

"Okay, I'm ready to tackle this beast," I proclaimed, and I ripped into the shrink-wrap.

After the bird was fully exposed, I noticed the corner of a bag sticking out of his rear end. "Hey, somebody hid something inside our turkey."

Maggie came over to take a look. "Oh, silly, nobody hid anything. Those are the giblets."

"The what?"

"Giblets! You know, some of the inside parts of the turkey."

"What am I supposed to do with them?"

"Well, I think you can make things with them, like stuffing and gravy."

"Hold on a minute. I don't ever remember Grandma putting giblets in her gravy. That just doesn't sound right."

I dried my hands, grabbed my dictionary, and looked up giblets. According to Mr. Webster, "Giblets are the edible offal of a fowl including the heart, gizzard, liver, and other visceral organs."

I nearly fainted.

"I'm sorry, Maggie, but no giblets will ever be eaten in my house or in my presence. I hope that's not a deal breaker."

"I think I can live with that," she replied.

I returned to the turkey, shoved my hand up his butt, and pulled out the bag of giblets. For curiosity's sake, I cut open the bag to take a look.

I shouldn't have done that. There are just some things that ought not be seen.

Sure enough, the inner plumbing of Tom Turkey spewed forth onto my countertop—and something else too.

A stiff piece of grisly meat about six inches long sat there staring me in the face.

"Holy crap!" I exclaimed. "Come here and look at this! That looks like—No! Surely they wouldn't that in the bag!"

"No, silly," Maggie replied. "That's his neck."

"This is just wrong in so many ways."

After disposing of the offending offal, I turned my attention to the cooking instructions I had pulled off the Internet.

Step one: Preheat oven to 325 degrees and select a three-to-four-inch roaster pan with lid. Cooking time: fifteen minutes per pound.

Step one seemed pretty easy.

Step two: For golden brown skin, spread butter evenly and season to taste with salt, pepper, garlic, or rosemary.

No problem.

I dipped into the "I Can't Believe It's Not Butter" tub and under Maggie's watchful eye started lathering the bird's ample breasts.

"Hmm, this feels kind of good," I murmured and gave Maggie my sly, "whadda you think" look.

"Don't even think about it, buster," she shot back.

"Okay, okay, I'll be good. Can you get me the salt and pepper and see what's in my spice rack?"

"Nothing here but crab boil and taco seasoning. But you do have salt and pepper."

"Well, it says 'season to taste,' and we both love tacos. How about we make Mexicali Turkey? I'll bet nobody's tried that before."

Maggie didn't disagree, so I liberally coated the buttered breasts with salt, pepper, and Old El Paso, and he was ready for step three, bake and baste.

"What about the stuffing? Aren't you going to make stuffing?"

"Oh yeah, stuffing. I almost forgot. How do you make it?" Seeing the blank look on Maggie's face, I muttered, "Well, back to the Internet."

After an exhaustive search, we discovered there were two methods of stuffing preparation, pan and bird. We went back to the kitchen and took a look up Tom's rear end.

"Isn't that where the offal came from?" I asked. Getting an affirmative nod from Maggie, I made an executive decision on the spot. "Pan it is."

Maggie didn't argue.

Besides, I couldn't ever remember my grandma digging stuffing out of the turkey's butt.

Satisfied with our preparation thus far, we plopped the bird in the oven and turned our attention to the stuffing.

Just then, the phone rang.

"Hi, Walt, it's Jerry. I think we may have a problem. There's a horrible smell coming from the basement. I'm afraid we might have a sewer backup."

Wonderful! Where am I going to find a plumber on Thanksgiving Day?

"Thanks, Jerry. I'll check it out. See you in a few hours."

I gave Willie a call.

"Willie, Jerry just called and said he thought our sewer might be backing up. Could you go take a look?"

"Well, hell, Mr. Walt, I'se right in de middle of cookin' my dish fo' de party, but sho, I'll take a look.

Hang on. I be right back."

"Evating looks okay to me. I don't see no problem."

"Thanks, Willie. See you later."

Relieved, I turned my attention back to the stuffing.

"Okay, it says to chop up onion and celery and sauté in melted butter. Let's see what's in the vegetable bin."

I had an onion, but the only other green thing was a head of lettuce.

"Aren't celery and lettuce in the same food group?" I asked. "I mean, they're both green and both a vegetable."

How could anyone argue with logic like that?

So we chopped up the onion and lettuce, and while they were boiling in the butter, we checked out the next ingredient, bread. More precisely, stuffing bread.

"What's stuffing bread?"

Another blank look.

I checked the breadbox and found a loaf of Wonder white bread fortified with vitamins and minerals.

"If we use this in our stuffing, doesn't it then become 'stuffing bread' by definition?"

Again, how could one argue with the logic?

So we cut the Wonder Bread in little cubes and added them to our boiling vegetable mix per the instructions.

The next step was add two cups of stock. "What's stock?" I wondered.

"Well, I think it's some kind of meat juice or gravy that comes in a can. I remember seeing cans of beef stock and chicken stock on the grocery shelf next to the soups."

We looked in the cabinet and found a can of Campbell's Beef Barley soup and a can of Campbell's Creamy Chicken Noodle soup.

"Since this is a fowl dish, I vote we go with the chicken noodle."

More culinary logic.

We opened the can, and sure enough, there was a creamy liquid.

"Looks like stock to me," I said.

"You going to drain it?"

"Why? Aren't bread and noodles almost the same thing? We've got a huge crowd coming today. This will add a little more body to the dish."

So into the pan went the soup.

The final step was to add poultry seasoning. Having already exposed the deficiencies in my spice rack, we knew the only thing left was crab boil. We looked at each other.

"What do you think?" I asked.

"Well, it's going to be pretty bland without some kind of seasoning."

So into the pot it went.

After mixing the gooey mess, we plopped it in a baking pan. Ready for the oven.

So far, so good.

The remainder of the morning was spent with last-minute cleaning, showering, shaving, and makeup sandwiched around our hourly basting duties.

The directions said to remove the lid during the final hour of cooking to ensure a golden brown skin. So off came the lid.

Our creative recipes had produced a rather unusual aroma that permeated the apartment. There was the essence of Taco Bell laced with a hint of Joe's Crab Shack. Not exactly what I remembered from Grandma's kitchen.

By twelve thirty, it was time for the bird to come out of the oven.

Beautiful!

Guests would be arriving soon, so it was time for the final preparations.

Then it hit me. Gravy!

I can't ever remember a Thanksgiving without turkey gravy.

Okay, think. How did Grandma make gravy?

I remembered seeing her add three ingredients: milk, flour, and the greasy stuff out of the bottom of the turkey pan.

We have all of that—I think.

We pulled Tom out of the pan, and several inches of rich, greasy turkey broth covered the bottom of the pan.

I went to the cabinet to look for flour and came up empty. I couldn't remember when I had bought flour. I don't bake.

But there on the shelf, next to my Top Ramen noodles, was my answer—Aunt Jemima.

Okay, so it was pancake mix, but flour is flour, right? I kept dumping Aunt Jemima in the turkey grease until I had a thick brown paste. I put the pan on the stove and added milk. I was ready to cook it down to a rich, smooth texture. It made my mouth water.

Just then, there was a knock on the door. Our first guest.

"Sweetie, can you get that?" Maggie called. "I'm almost done in the bathroom."

"No problem."

I wiped my hands and opened the front door. Vince was the first to arrive, bearing a big box from the Pie Pantry.

"Pumpkin. Hope you like it," he said as he handed me the box and shook my hand.

"It wouldn't be Thanksgiving without it," I replied. "Come on in and have a seat. We're just finishing up in the kitchen."

I was just closing the door when I saw eighty-three-year-old Bernice coming down the hall with a package under her arm.

"Hi, Walt. I feel kind of bad bringing this." She handed me a package of frozen rolls. "I've been under the weather and didn't get to the store, but I found these in my freezer."

"Hot rolls sound yummy. The oven's still hot. We'll pop 'em right on in. Vince is in the living room. Go chat with him."

126

As I headed to the kitchen with the rolls and pie, I couldn't help but notice that the expiration date fell somewhere during George Bush's first term as president.

Oh well, age is relevant, isn't it?

I entered the kitchen and suddenly realized I'd forgotten about the gravy. It was boiling furiously in the turkey pan. I think I was supposed to be stirring it, but it was too late now. It was already thick.

I heard another knock on the door and hoped that Maggie could get it. I was balancing a huge turkey pan full of hot gravy, trying to figure out how to get it in a bowl without scalding myself.

Just then Ox entered the kitchen.

"Hey, buddy. Brought you a pie. You like pumpkin, don't you? Here, let me give you a hand with that pan."

Together we hoisted the bubbling turkey pan off the stove and began pouring the contents in my big popcorn bowl.

"What is this stuff?" Ox asked.

"Gravy!"

"What are those lumpy things? I don't ever remember seeing gravy with lumpy things."

"Well, this is pancake gravy. It's supposed to have lumps. So just shut up."

Before Ox could reply, Mary burst through the door carrying a box from the Price Chopper bakery department.

"Hey, Mr. Walt, I brought us a—Damn! Where did all these other pumpkin pies come from?"

Ox and I just looked at each other. We were both scared to answer.

"Well, hell, I thought I was doing something special. Guess not. But at least I brought some topping for my pie." She proudly displayed a huge carton of Cool Whip.

I was about to compliment her for her thoughtfulness when I noticed that the label read 'strawberry.'

Mary saw it at the same time.

"Damn, damn, damn. I grabbed the wrong carton."

I grabbed the pie and the Cool Whip, handed them to Ox, and ushered Mary out of the kitchen.

"I bet it will be great," I said. "We get to try something new."

Maggie had just welcomed Jerry and the professor who, thank heavens, hadn't brought a pie. He came bearing two huge jugs of Arbor Mist peach chardonnay.

And what did Jerry bring? You guessed it—a pie.

I threw Bernice's rolls in the oven and joined our guests.

The last to arrive was Willie. He was carrying a huge covered casserole dish.

"Whatcha got there Willie?" I asked as he set the bowl on the table.

"It's a surprise. It's sumptin' I bet youall's nevva had befo."

Then it will fit right in with the rest of this meal, I thought.

"Professor, would you please pour the wine while Maggie and I get the rest of the food?"

While I was carrying the bird and gravy to the table, Maggie was pulling Bernice's rolls from the oven.

We both looked at the pitiful little wads of dough on the cookie sheet.

"Aren't these things supposed to get bigger?" Maggie asked.

"It's a long story," I replied. "I'll explain later."

With the food on the table, I invited our guests to take their seats.

Bernice, bless her heart, was the last to sit. As she plopped into the chair, a resounding pwspoooooosppthh came from the vicinity of her backside.

We all sat in utter silence and embarrassment as a look of horror spread across her face.

Finally, Jerry couldn't hold it any longer. His devilish smile turned into a grin and finally erupted in uncontrolled giggling.

A mortified Bernice was gingerly exploring her nether parts. Her horror turned to bewilderment and then to relief as she produced a flat rubber bag, and it dawned her that the offensive noise was a product of Jerry's whoopie cushion and not her incontinence.

A round of applause erupted as Bernice deftly turned and whacked Jerry on the head with the offensive latex.

"Hey, it could have been worse," Jerry quipped. "Did you hear the one about the granny?"

We all rolled our eyes and sighed.
"Okay, just one. I promise.

An accident really uncanny
befell an unfortunate granny.
She sat down on a chair
while her false teeth were there
and bit herself right on the fanny!

What did I think was going to happen when I invited a joker to Thanksgiving dinner?

I was trying to restore order to the table when Jerry lifted the lid on Willie's covered casserole dish.

"I've been curious to see what—**Oh, sweet mother of God, what is that smell?**"

A foul stench quickly spread across the table. "Walt, that's that stink I called you about this morning. You know—the sewer smell."

A crestfallen Willie looked around the table and saw the look of obvious disgust in his friends' faces.

"Dem's chitlins. I thought maybe you all like to try some soul food."

"What are chitlins?" Maggie asked.

The professor came to the rescue. "Chitlins are the boiled or fried small intestines of pigs. In slavery days, when hogs were slaughtered, the masters kept the good meat and gave what was left over to the slaves."

"Well, that certainly explains the sewer smell," Jerry replied.

"Hey, dem's ho made. I guess you all not interested in a new cultural experience."

"Don't you mean homemade?" the Professor corrected.

"No, I means ho made! Maxine came over dis mornin' and helped me cook 'em."

"Where's Maxine now?" I asked.

"She downstairs. She didn't think nobody would want her around."

I looked around the table. Nods and winks were everywhere.

"Willie, why don't you go get Maxine? We'd love to have her join us. After all, we've got plenty of clown plates."

"You sure?" he asked.

I nodded, and Willie headed to the basement.

When Willie and Maxine returned and we were all seated, I looked at our diverse little group marveling at how, during the past year, circumstances in each of our lives had brought us to this moment.

I looked at the food on the table: Mexicali turkey, Wonder Bread crab paste, Aunt Jemima gravy, hockey puck rolls, chitlins, and enough pumpkin pie with strawberry Cool Whip to feed the Mormon Tabernacle Choir.

And, of course, we had the perfect wine pairing, Arbor Mist. It goes good with everything.

Not exactly a traditional Thanksgiving, but I wouldn't have traded it for anything in the world.

To honor the occasion, we joined hands around the table, and each, in turn, shared one thing they were thankful for in their lives.

Maxine was last, and her comments summed it up for the rest of us.

"I'se thankful dat I found some folks dat can look past what I am and accept me fo who I am."

We could all say an amen to that.

We all stuffed ourselves with turkey and pumpkin pie, those being the only dishes that were actually edible, and spent the remainder of the day enjoying each other's company and reliving shared experiences of the past year.

Traditionally, Thanksgiving signals the start of the Christmas season. Many events are scheduled on and around Thanksgiving to launch the holiday festivities.

The Country Club Plaza lighting ceremony and the mayor's Christmas tree draw huge crowds, but in our Midtown Kansas City neighborhood, the main event is the opening of the live nativity scene at Pastor Bob's Community Church.

Some carpenter in years past had constructed a wooden manger consisting of a backdrop, a cradle for the baby Jesus, and a small fenced area for the live animals. Life-size statues of Mary, Joseph, the angel, and three shepherds were accompanied by a live sheep and a donkey.

Obviously livestock kept penned up for a month needed care. This was provided by Moses Thacker. He was a farmer from rural Missouri. He had retired and moved to Kansas City to be near his family. Missing the farm life, he had volunteered to care for the animals, bringing them food and water and cleaning the stall daily.

Over the years, the nativity scene had experienced some problems. Vandals of both the two-legged and four-legged kind couldn't seem to leave it alone. City creatures of the night, such as raccoons and large rats, were constantly foraging in the animals' food, and once a possum was found curled up in the cradle with the baby Jesus.

Kansas City, like other large metropolitan areas, has its population of taggers: that's guys who paint things on the side of buildings and on bridge overpasses. One year the taggers painted the sheep red and green and hung a big Christmas bell from its tail.

Old Moses was up to the task. He cordoned off a huge section of lawn surrounding the nativity and set the area with snare traps. This area came to be known as the DMZ, and anyone or thing who dared to enter was found the next morning in Moses's snares. The critters were carted off by Animal Control, and the taggers were carted off to jail.

We tidied up the kitchen, grabbed our coats, and headed to Pastor Bob's First Community Church.

We should have started earlier, as a huge crowd had already gathered and was pressing against the rope to the DMZ. No one wants to miss this event.

Even the Presbyterians show up.

Fortunately, we have Mary. Over the years, she has developed a technique for parting a crowd and worming through. She always gets dirty looks, but who's gonna hassle an old lady?

So Mary did her thing, pulling all of us behind her in single file until we reached the rope barricade.

And there, in all its glory, was the First Community Church live nativity scene.

Floodlights shone on the holy figures and the livestock. City fathers were present to pontificate on the significance of the event, and Pastor Bob of the First Community Church stood proudly looking on.

Suddenly a collective gasp went up from the onlookers. I craned my neck to see what had diverted everyone's attention, and my eyes were immediately drawn to the donkey who was obviously a male.

It was at this most inopportune time that he had apparently become aroused, and his weenie was extended so far it almost dragged the ground.

In school there was a boy who the other kids nicknamed "Donkey Dick." At the time, in my innocence, I thought it was an insult. Actually, I guess it was more of a compliment.

This was an opportunity that Mary couldn't pass up. She turned to Willie standing at her side.

"Willie, you didn't tell me your brother was in the play this year. That is your brother, isn't it? The family resemblance is quite obvious."

Most people would have been offended. Willie just grinned.

As if that weren't enough action for one ceremony, the sheep suddenly hunched his back, bleated, and dropped a load right there in the manger.

Little girls giggled. Boys hooted. The elders were appropriately shocked.

Happy holidays! Christmas had officially started in Kansas City.

CHAPTER 10

Manny Delano was relieved to be able to bring good news to Salvatore Lorenzo. "We've got the votes, Mr. L. We'll get the green light at the next City Council meeting."

"You're certain? I don't want no surprises."

"Absolutely! It took some arm twisting, but those photos of Councilman Higgins with Rosalina clinched the deal. The urban renewal project is in the bag."

"Very well then. Once the project hits the papers every Tom, Dick and Harry will be sticking their noses into our business. We need to make sure our asses are covered. Call a meeting. I want everybody there, Emile, Michael, Connie and the cop. The Foxy Lady, Friday night. Any questions?"

"No Sir, I'll see that everyone's there."

After our memorable holiday, it was back to work.

At the squad meeting I was disappointed to learn that no new leads had developed in our case. Some creative genius had dubbed the investigation into the blighted, abandoned neighborhood 'Operation Desperation,' and the name stuck.

We had suspects but no evidence. We had crime but no motive.

Then one day, out of the blue, an article on the front page of the Kansas City Star brought the elusive motive into clear focus.

The headline read, *"City Councilman Manny Delano Set to Unveil Urban Renewal Proposal for Eastside Neighborhood."* It went on to say that Councilman Delano, appalled by the blighted neighborhood in his district, was working with state and federal officials on a joint venture to infuse new life and new business into this troubled area.

Such a program was nothing new to Kansas City. Previous urban renewal programs had met with great success.

The old garment district sat abandoned for years after the industry was outsourced to China. The old multistoried factory buildings were converted to elegant loft apartments and are homes today for Kansas City's yuppie elite.

As the Kansas City gentry fled to the suburbs and the new sprawling mega-malls, the downtown business district saw store after store close their doors. After years of downward spiral, a massive renewal project produced the Sprint Center sports/event arena and the rebirth of what's now known as the Power and Light District. The once seldom-visited area is now a beehive of activity, and the bars, restaurants, and clubs are often standing room only.

Dozens of square blocks of Midtown Kansas City had become blighted and run down, and crime was on the rise until the initiation of the "Glover Plan,"

137

named for the industrious city councilman who brought the plan to fruition. Whole city blocks of blighted homes were purchased by the city, demolished, and replaced with giant anchor chain stores.

As realtors, Maggie and I had been in the middle of that action as entrepreneurs and speculators came from far and wide and snatched up the homes and apartment buildings on the fringes of the new project. Millions of rehabilitation dollars poured into the area, and Councilman Glover was a hero.

So what was different about the announcement of a new urban renewal project on the east side?

Maybe it was the fact that the entire blighted area was owned by one entity, Eastside Properties.

Millions of city, county, and federal taxpayer dollars would flow into the coffers of a corporation, which is a subsidiary of an offshore company located in the Bahamas, whose principals are probably members of the Lorenzo and Mancuso families and the Italian mob.

We had already determined that Riverfront Realty, which had brokered the dozens of sales to Eastside Properties, was part of the Lorenzo empire. But none of this would have been initiated by the mob unless they had assurances and prior knowledge that the urban renewal project was forthcoming.

It was obvious that mob influence and control had permeated City Hall.

But to what extent?

It didn't take a genius to figure out that Councilman DeLano was part of the plan, but where was the proof?

To the average citizen of Kansas City, all that was needed to endorse Delano's proclamation in the *Star* was a drive through the blighted neighborhood. Here was another hero in the making.

Ox and I had finished our shift and were ready to clock out when Captain Short approached us in the squad room.

"I'd like a word with the two of you in my office before you leave," he said and abruptly walked away.

Ox and I just stood there looking like dummies.

"Well, what did we do now?" I asked.

Ox shrugged his shoulders in bewilderment. "I guess we'll find out."

As we entered Captain Short's office, he glanced over our shoulders and said, "Did anyone see you come in?"

I looked at Ox, and he shook his head.

"I don't think so, sir. We were the last ones out of the locker room."

"Good. Shut the door and have a seat."

This couldn't be good.

"Gentlemen, we have a problem. I'm sure you've heard about Councilman DeLano's urban renewal project. We're sure the whole thing has been orchestrated by the mob, but we have no proof.

"To make matters worse, we are now certain that there is a leak here in our department. One or more of our officers are on their payroll. That's the only way they could have known about our operations. I just don't know whom I can trust."

"What can we do, sir?" I asked.

"Our patrols in the blighted area noticed an anomaly. All the businesses in the vicinity were closed or burned except one, The Foxy Lady.

"We grew suspicious when we received no complaints from the bar's patrons or owners. Why were they the only business not being harassed? A records check indicated that the building was owned by another dummy company with ties to the Bahama corporation. They didn't need to harass anyone. They already owned it.

"It's a two-story brick building with offices on the top floor and The Foxy Lady on the ground floor. We think the offices may be the mob's headquarters."

"So do you want Ox and I to keep an eye on the place?"

There was a long pause.

"We need more than that. We need someone inside the bar to watch and record who's coming and going."

"That's not a problem. Ox, Vince, and I have done undercover work before."

I turned to Ox for confirmation and was surprised to see his face buried in his meaty hands.

"What?"

Ox and the captain exchanged worried looks. They obviously knew something I didn't.

"What?" I asked again.

The captain looked at Ox. "You tell him," he said.

Ox just stared at me.

"What, damn it?"

"The Foxy Lady is a tranny bar."

"A tra—No! Absolutely not! I've been a john in a strip club and a homosexual in a gay bar, but there's no way in hell you're getting me into a dress!"

"Walt, you're all I've got."

"Why me?"

"First and most importantly, I trust you and Ox. You and I go all the way back to high school. Someone out there is dirty, and I just don't know who it is. Second, look around. How do you think Ox would look in a dress? Most of the guys in the squad are built like tanks. You, not so much. You've got the perfect build for the job."

"But I'm so old," I protested.

"It's amazing what a little skillfully applied makeup will hide."

"You've really thought this through, haven't you?"

"Walt, if there was any other way, I wouldn't ask you to do this."

I sat in silence. I tried to conjure up an image of myself in drag and was horrified at what I saw. Why me? Haven't I been humiliated enough?

I remembered my conversation with Pastor Bob. His soul-searching words rang in my head: "You all

141

done cleaning up the streets? No more bad guys to catch? Or maybe you figure you've caught your share and now it's somebody else's turn?"

Only there wasn't anyone else.

Then there it was.

Why did I get involved with the City Retiree Action Patrol in the first place? Wasn't it because I believed old guys like me were in a position to make a unique contribution and really make a difference?

Put up or shut up.

Nobody said it would be easy.

Ox and the captain never uttered a word as I battled my internal demons. They sat quietly awaiting my decision.

With a sigh of resignation, I addressed my friends. "Okay, how do we do this?"

My relieved captain was grinning from ear to ear. "I knew I could count on you."

Am I really that predictable?

"Here's the thing. No one else can know about this operation. We know there is a leak, and if word gets back to the mob that you're undercover, no one's going to come around. And even worse, I don't even want to think about what they'd do to you."

With my recent brush with death still painfully vivid, I didn't want to think about it either.

"If we have to keep this under wraps, who's going to transform me into a drag queen?"

"Well, I was hoping maybe Maggie could help."

Oh swell! This just keeps getting worse and worse.

It's bad enough that I have to wear a dress and makeup, and now they want my girlfriend to be my fashion consultant. How much mortification can one man take?

"Just hang on to your receipts and we'll reimburse you after this is all over."

"Shopping! I have to go shopping too?"

"Well, you've got to have a wardrobe and makeup and accessories and—"

"And what?"

"And your electronic surveillance equipment. We're going to fit you with a mike so Ox can keep track of you and a big brooch that has a mini-cam to record who comes and goes. We'll need hard, physical evidence when we go to court."

We hammered out the remaining details of the operation, and as we stood to leave, the captain grabbed my hand.

"Walt, thank you. This means a lot to me."

I knew even less about the transvestite community than I did the gay community, so I figured I had better do some research.

My only exposure to this other world was newspaper ads I had seen in the entertainment section promoting the latest attractions at the Jewel Box Lounge. This famous lounge had been a part of Kansas City's nightclub scene since the 1930s.

Female impersonators from all over the country performed to packed houses. I remember seeing ads for acts such as the 'Gender Benders,' and even straight couples marveled at the extravagant productions.

I went to the library and found several books on the subject: *Recollections of a Part Time Lady* and *Transvestism Today*.

But the eye-opener was a book titled *A Pictorial History of the Art of Female Impersonation.*

Wow!

As I perused the photos of guys in drag, I couldn't help but be impressed. Some of them were gorgeous! I knew there were men who found pleasure in wearing ladies' garments, and I had seen movies of male prostitutes in drag, but this was a whole new side of things I hadn't seen.

I was skeptical about checking out the book from the library. I think they keep a record of what everybody reads somewhere, and I wasn't sure I wanted this one on my reading list, but I thought it might give Maggie and me some ideas.

I gave Maggie a call and asked if I could come by her place after work. I even promised to pick up some subs at Quizno's.

How could a girl turn down an offer like that?

Supper, such as it was, went quite well.

After she had told me about her day, it was time to face the inevitable.

"So what exciting things did you do today?" she asked.

"I've got something to talk to you about, and I don't want you to interrupt me or ask any questions until I'm completely finished, okay?"

Her look of bewilderment turned to astonishment and finally to amusement as I laid the whole story on the table. I could tell she was doing her best to keep from laughing.

"You think this is funny, don't you?"

"Well, yeah!"

Not exactly the reaction I was expecting.

"I've always wanted a girlfriend I could shop with and share makeup secrets. This is going to be fun."

Yeah, a real hoot!

For reasons I'll never understand, Maggie attacked her role with a vengeance. She composed a list of all the accoutrements we would need for my transformation and then started checking off items she had on hand.

Apparently women are loath to throw away makeup, even if it's stuff they haven't used for ages, and Maggie produced a plastic tub full of jars and tubes that she pronounced as perfect.

Evidently the same rules apply with selected articles of clothing. Maggie is a svelte 120 pounds now, but sometime in the distant past, she must have been a few pounds heavier. A box from the spare room closet labeled 'save' contained frilly relics from her heftier days.

After comparing items on hand with her inventory list, Maggie was satisfied that the only articles we were lacking were a dress, shoes, and a wig.

The next day we would shop.

Just to be sure everything was right, Maggie insisted on a trial fitting of the undergarments and proceeded to pull a pair of lacy panties, a bra, and pantyhose from her stash.

"Okay, buster, strip."

On more than one occasion, those very words from Maggie were music to my ears.

Not this time.

I'm definitely not a prude, especially when it comes to Maggie, but I'm more accustomed to us getting nekkid together.

"I'll just do this in here," I said as I grabbed the panties and bra and headed for the bathroom.

As I slipped off my BVDs and picked up the panties, I encountered my first dilemma. Is there a front and a back to these things? How can you tell without a fly?

Then I saw the little tag and assumed that was the backside.

So far, so good.

Next came the bra.

My previous experience with this garment had focused on removal rather than installation, and I nearly dislocated my shoulders trying to hook the damn thing behind my back. I concluded that one had to be either a contortionist or double-jointed to master this, and I, being neither of those, gave up and retreated to the bedroom. I explained my problem to Maggie, and she gave me a quick lesson on "hook in front and rotate to the back."

146

A valuable lesson.

Since my chest wasn't exactly designed to fill the size C cups, Maggie augmented my bosom with wadded-up pantyhose.

While in the pantyhose pile, she selected a dark pair she described as 'smoke.'

"Try these on. I think they're dark enough that you won't have to shave your legs."

"You're damn right I won't. That's where I draw the line. I'll just tell people I'm from Sweden."

She handed me the pantyhose, and I looked at the tiny ball of material.

"That's not big enough for one leg. How am I going to get two, plus my butt, in there?"

"Just put them on. Trust me. They expand."

I sat on the bed and started pulling them up one leg at a time, and sure enough, they did expand.

But as I stood, I was beginning to get signals from Mr. Winkie and the boys.

"Kind of crowded in here," I complained.

"Yeah," she quipped. "Pantyhose are a lot like cheap hotels—no ballroom."

She was having way too much fun with this.

Now that I was all decked out in my bra and pantyhose, Maggie stepped back to take a look at her handiwork.

"Not bad," she declared. "In fact, I think I'm getting a little turned on."

The evening wasn't a total loss after all.

Maggie had no appointments the next morning, so we headed to the Salvation Army Thrift Store to complete my outfit.

I've never been much of a shopper. Guys don't have to be. I have two kinds of pants, dress and casual. If I need a pair, I go to the store, grab my size off the rack, and check out. No need to try it on. It's exactly like the one I'm replacing.

But I'd never bought a dress.

As we rummaged through the racks, Maggie would pull one out and hold it up in front of me. I found myself saying stuff like, "No, that's just not right for me," or, "I think we can do better."

What was happening to me?

I actually tried one on and asked Maggie if it made my butt look big.

Where did that come from?

Finally, I found one that felt just right. It was the perfect shade of brown to bring out the color in my eyes and while not slutty, was just tight enough to accent my figure.

My God, what did I just say?

Our next stop was the wig rack. There was a huge selection of both colors and lengths. I had always heard that blondes have more fun, so I tried on a saucy blonde pageboy with bangs.

I looked like Phyllis Diller.

148

I told Maggie I needed something shoulder length, fuller, with more body.

I was starting to scare myself!

I finally settled on a dark auburn with flirty bangs that matched my dress perfectly.

Shoes were a different story.

I wear a size nine and a half, which is average for a guy. By comparison, Ox wears a size twelve. But finding a woman's shoe in a low heel that would fit a guy proved to be a challenge. We had to hit three thrift stores before we found something I could walk in.

'Walk in' might be too generous. 'Wobble in' would be more accurate.

My new footwear sported two-inch heels, nothing remarkable for the ladies but a definite challenge for me.

Maggie and I love to dance, and we watch *Dancing with the Stars* on TV. I had always marveled at how the lady professionals could execute all those fast and intricate steps wearing four-inch spike heels. I have even greater respect for them now.

Walking on my ankles in my two-inch heels was reminiscent of my first experience on ice skates. It was not a pretty sight.

Our shopping concluded, and I called Ox and told him to meet at Maggie's apartment with the surveillance equipment.

After lunch, Maggie suggested we start getting my makeup on. She said that we might run into some issues. I wondered what she meant by that.

149

We sat at her kitchen table, and she spread her whole array of jars and tubes and brushes.

"When did you shave last?"

"This morning."

"Go do it again. I can only cover up just so much."

I shaved, and when I returned she had made her selections.

"Okay, foundation goes on first." She started smearing this light-brown pasty cream all over my face.

"Now the eyebrows." She started drawing on my forehead with some kind of grease pencil.

"Hold really still or I'll poke your eye out." She out-lined my eyelids with a little pencil thing.

"Now don't blink." She came at me with some kind of pliers that she clamped on my eyelashes.

"Now for the lip liner and lipstick." She coated my mouth with "cinnamon rose."

It occurred to me that it was much more fun getting the lipstick off her mouth than her putting it on me.

"Now for a little blush to give you some color and a pat of powder so you don't shine."

Oh good. I really don't want to shine.

She stood back to admire her handiwork.

"I'm afraid that's as good as it's going to get."

Just what every gal wants to hear.

I looked in the mirror and yikes! I looked like a cross between Ronald McDonald, Howdy Doody, and Raggedy Ann.

"It'll be better with your wig on," she said.

I certainly hoped so.

Just then, there was a knock on the door.

Maggie opened the door, and Ox strode in with an armful of electronics. He gave Maggie a hug, took a look at me, and to his credit pretended that nothing was different. I noticed, though, that he quickly turned away and headed for the kitchen with his box. As he went through the door, I know I heard him snicker. I know he did.

He returned, composed, and with an air of professionalism said, "I see you're ready for our evening out, Mrs. Williams."

Maggie had witnessed the exchange and finally could hold it no longer. She burst into an uncontrollable fit of laughter that sent Ox over the edge, and the two of them collapsed on the couch.

As I watched their frivolity at my expense, my first reaction was hurt. Then I felt a wave of resentment. But as I was about to lash out in protest, I saw myself in the mirror, and I caved in too.

If you can't beat 'em, join 'em.

Once the laughter subsided, it was time to get to work.

In the privacy of the bedroom, I put on my lace panties, pantyhose, and bra (hook in front, rotate to the back).

Ox had to bite his lip hard as he hooked up my electronics.

Soon a small battery pack was pinned into the waist of my pantyhose, and a wire attached to a tiny microphone ran from my navel up through my bra and out my cleavage, such as it was.

Another wire with a miniature speaker ran from the battery pack down and under my crotch and up between my butt crack, up the back of my dress, and under my wig and into my ear.

I felt like I had been assimilated by the Borg. If you're a *Star Trek* fan, you'll understand.

Maggie helped me slip my dress over my head, fasten my belt, and don my wig.

After a long look, she said, "We've got a problem."

"What?"

"Your waddle."

"My what?"

"Your waddle. You know, that flap of skin that hangs down under your chin."

"You've never mentioned it before."

"You've never been a girl before."

She had me there.

She went to the closet and came back with a silk scarf.

"There. That should do it."

I slipped on my heels and took a look in the full-length mirror.

"I look like Tina Turner on steroids," I murmured.

"Then 'Tina' it is," they said in unison.

My last accessory was the big brooch mini-cam that I could activate with a remote I would carry in my purse.

We were ready for The Foxy Lady.

152

The plan was simple enough.

We needed evidence to tie Councilman DeLano and Riverfront Realty to the mob and, even more important to us, to find the dirty cop who was selling us out.

We drove through the neighborhood in an old, beat-up unmarked car.

The two-story building with The Foxy Lady on the ground floor appeared to have both a front and rear entrance, and the upper story was accessed from a separate door on the street level.

My job was to patronize the lounge, keeping an eye out for our persons of interest on the inside while Ox sat in the unmarked across the street in an old boarded-up gas station. I had my mini-cam brooch, and Ox was equipped with an SLR with a telephoto lens and night-vision filter.

Were we high-tech or what?

Ox dropped me off a few blocks from the bar, and I wobbled off to my assignment.

I entered the lounge and found a table near the front where I could see not only the bar patrons but also anyone who might be using the second-story entrance. I surveyed the patrons scattered throughout the lounge, and I have to admit that I was disappointed.

After reading *The Pictorial History of the Art of Female Impersonation*, I had expectations of men decked out in glamorous sequined dresses and Dolly Parton wigs.

Not even close.

As I surveyed the crowd, I actually wondered if I was overdressed.

A guy came over in a tacky French maid outfit and took my drink order. He gave me the once-over, winked, and walked away.

I guessed that I passed muster.

For a while no one seemed to pay much attention to me, but finally a stocky guy in a polka-dot outfit came to my table. He looked like Yogi Berra dressed as Imogene Coca.

"Mind if I have a seat?"

"Help yourself."

"You're new at this, aren't you?"

Was it really that obvious?

"How could you tell?" I asked.

"Your legs. They're spread apart. Ladies sit with their legs together."

I looked down, and sure enough, I was flashing everyone in the bar.

I quickly closed the gap.

"Sorry about that. Guess I have a lot to learn."

"Not a problem. You'll get the hang of it. By any chance are you looking for some action?"

Oh boy!

I could hear Ox snickering in my earphone.

"Well, thanks for asking, but actually I'm just trying to get a feel for things, you know, taking it kinda slow."

"I totally understand. When you're ready, I'll be around." He left my table and moved back to the bar.

A real gentleman—er, lady, I guess.

From my vantage point, I could also see down a narrow hallway with three doors. I figured two of them were bathrooms and was curious about the third.

I headed down the hall noting that the bathrooms were clearly marked 'he-he' and 'she-he.' I guess you gotta know the code.

The third door said 'private.' I looked around, and seeing no one, I turned the knob and took a peek. It was an inside stairway that led to the second-story offices.

"Hey, buddy, the sign says 'private.' Can't you read?"

I turned and was face to face with a huge goombah with a crooked nose. Where did he come from?

"Oh, sorry. This is my first time here. I was just looking for the men's—uh—I mean ladies' room."

After a long look, he finally said, "That way." He pointed a meaty finger down the hall.

If I didn't have to go before, I certainly did then.

I made my way down the hall and was faced with a decision. I concluded that in my current attire, I was probably a she-he.

Finding myself alone, I whispered to Ox, "That was a close one. But I did find an inside entrance to the second floor. Any activity out there?"

"Not yet. You be careful. Don't do anything stupid."

Who, me?

At that point I realized that Maggie had skipped a vital part of my training. I knew Mr. Winkie was buried down there somewhere, but how does one access one's equipment without completely disrobing?

After a lot of hiking up and pulling down, I finally located Mr. Winkie. He looked pretty forlorn. I hoped there was no permanent damage.

I resumed my vigil and soon noticed a big Lincoln Town Car pull to the curb. Michael and Constance Lorenzo made a hasty exit and headed for the upstairs door, and the Town Car pulled away.

"Ox, did you get that?" I whispered.

"Got it!"

Just then the back door opened, and the goon that accosted me in the hall and another slimeball headed my way. I reached into my purse and activated my mini-cam as they headed for the hallway and up the stairs.

"Who just got out of that car?" I heard in my earpiece.

I was so wrapped up in my cinematic duties that I hadn't seen the Caddie Escalade pull up in front.

I looked out of the window, and bingo, the big fish.

"It's Councilman Delano," I whispered.

"Got him," Ox replied.

With the arrival of Riverfront Realty, the councilman, and the mob goons, I figured a major strategy meeting was underway. Salvatore Lorenzo and Emile Mancuso had probably arrived earlier to prepare for their guests.

If only I could get close enough to hear what was going on, maybe we could wrap this thing up. We needed hard evidence, but how?

I didn't relish the idea of tangling with the Incredible Hulk again, but I needed to get close enough for my mike to pick up their conversation.

I headed for the hallway, paused, and put my ear to the door marked 'private.'

Hearing no sound, I gently eased the door open and heard muffled voices coming from above. If I could just slip up the stairs, I might be close enough to pick it up.

I reached in my purse and hit the remote for my mini-cam.

Then I heard footsteps heading toward the hallway. I quickly retraced my steps and made a dash for the first available door, the 'he-he.'

I slipped into a stall and stood quietly.

I heard the door open, a fly unzip, a fart, a grunt, and a tinkle as the guy relieved himself. Then I heard water running in the basin and finally the sound of the door opening and closing.

I figured I was in the clear.

Just as I reached for the door handle, I heard, "Damn! I left my—" and the door flew open.

I was staring into the face of Captain Harrington! We both just stood there, frozen in the moment.

His look of surprise changed to bewilderment as he gazed at the spectacle that confronted him, and then suddenly the bewilderment became concern and finally anger as he looked past the powder and lipstick and realized who was standing before him.

"You! You son-of-a-bitch!"

I tried to push past him, but he outweighed me by fifty pounds. He slammed me into the stall door, taking my breath away.

"Captain Harrington!" I gasped, hoping Ox would hear the exchange through the mike.

"You've been a pain in the ass since day one," he hissed. "But that's about to come to an end."

He twisted my arm behind my back and shoved me into the hall and up the stairs.

I had hoped to find out what was happening upstairs, but not exactly like this.

I should be more careful what I wish for.

He pushed me into a large conference room, and all the players were seated around a table.

"Look what I found downstairs," he bellowed.

"So what?" Salvatore Lorenzo retorted. "The whole bar is filled with trannies."

"Yeah, but this one's an undercover cop."

"He's probably not alone," Mancuso chimed in. "Check him for a wire."

Harrington patted me down and found the mike and earpiece, which he savagely yanked, driving the strategically placed wire forcefully up my butt.

I'm here to tell you that a phone wire wedgie is no fun.

"So what are we going to do?" Delano wailed. "We're so close. The council vote on the urban renewal project is just days away."

Harrington smacked the back of my head. "Before tonight, all they had were theories, no hard evidence. I'm betting it's just this old fart and his partner. We eliminate them and it's back to square one for the task force. We'll have the project locked up before they can regroup."

Lorenzo spoke up. "Okay then, Harrington. You take care of this creep, and I'll have my guys whack his partner. He has to be close by." He nodded his head, and the two goons went after Ox.

Harrington turned to me. "Okay, Grandpa, let's go. I've been looking forward to this." He slapped a pair of cuffs on my wrists and pushed me out the door and down the steps.

We exited through the rear entrance, and he shoved me in the backseat of an old four-door.

"Let's go somewhere quiet, and we'll get this over with real quick."

Harrington peeled out of the parking lot, and we headed south on Troost to Linwood Boulevard. I had no idea where he was taking me, but at least he was driving through an area I knew quite well.

He was moving at a good clip and barely hesitated at stop signs and intersections. But suddenly ahead we saw the flashing lights of an ambulance and fire truck, and a motorcycle cop was in the intersection directing traffic. He had no choice but to come to a dead stop, and I saw my chance.

Fortunately, he had cuffed my hands in front, a rookie mistake. I yanked the handle, and the door flew open. I bailed out of the car and took off across an open lot.

I was just a block away from Pastor Bob's Community Church, and I headed in that direction hoping to find sanctuary there.

I looked over my shoulder as I ran and saw Harrington pull to the curb about a block away and leap from the car.

At least I had a head start.

I ran up to the front door of the church and gave a tug—locked. I could see Harrington hot on my heels about a half block away.

I frantically looked around and saw the live nativity scene and sprinted in that direction.

There in the stable were the wise men and angels, and Joseph and Mary were kneeling by the manger. The sheep and donkey stood stoically, watching the world go by.

I suddenly recalled how many times I had seen perps hide from the cops right in plain sight, and it gave me an idea.

I rushed to the manger, stripped the Holy Mother of her blue hooded robe, and hid her body behind a bale of hay.

I figured since I was still in drag I had a chance, so I donned the blue robe and quietly knelt at the manger.

I secretly hoped there was no penalty in the afterlife for impersonating a holy figure.

I heard Harrington's footsteps coming near and figured that since I was already in a kneeling position, a little prayer wouldn't hurt.

Harrington came to a stop at the church. He tried the door as I had done, and finding it locked, he headed in my direction.

He paused a mere twenty feet from the manger and looked around. Finding no indication of my presence, he started to move away, probably thinking I had moved on.

I had been holding my breath, and as I saw him moving in the opposite direction, I felt a wave of relief wash over me.

But just at that moment, the donkey farted. It wasn't just a little toot. It was a bell ringer.

So forceful was the eruption that it frightened the pigeons roosting in the church eves, and they flew away in terror.

Harrington stopped short at the commotion and turned in my direction.

I too was startled and briefly lifted my head.

Our eyes met, and a big grin spread across the captain's face.

"Gotcha now, Grandpa." He drew his revolver and started in my direction.

I leaped to my feet and sprinted across the lawn, totally forgetting I was in Moses Thacker's DMZ. I heard a 'whup' and felt a sting as Moses's snare trap wrapped around my leg.

Harrington was right behind me. But just as he lifted his revolver, a second snare snapped, and Harrington fell in a heap.

We were both securely bound in the snares, but Harrington had the advantage. He still had his gun.

He was on the ground, but he twisted his body and aimed the big .45 in my direction.

I closed my eyes and was expecting the worst when I heard, "Drop it, Harrington."

I looked up, and Ox and Vince and seemingly half the squad were pointing their weapons at the captain.

Harrington laid his gun on the ground and began to weep. His career in law enforcement had come to an inglorious end.

Ox strolled to my side and looked at the spectacle on the ground, a sixty-six-year-old cop dressed in drag, wearing the hooded robe of the Holy Mother.

With a gleam in his eye, he quipped, "The Virgin Mary, I presume."

It would take months to sort through the details of the urban renewal scandal, but with the recordings from my mike and mini-cam, Ox's photos, and Captain Harrington's testimony, we had enough evidence for the grand jury to indict the Lorenzo and Mancuso families as well as Councilman Delano.

Many years ago the world found hope in a lowly manger. On this night, we found justice.

CHAPTER 11

Historically, when we bring a case to a successful conclusion, there is a short respite in which we can bask in the glow of our victory and congratulate one another on a job well done. But for me, the nightmare was not over.

On the night of Captain Harrington's arrest, as I lay trussed in Moses Thacker's snare, I was so relieved at just being alive that I didn't notice the dozens of cell phones busily snapping candid photos of the old dude in drag.

Imagine my consternation and humiliation when I arrived at the station and a pictorial display of my brief foray into transvestism was plastered on every wall and bulletin board.

While cops aren't generally known for their sensitivity, they are usually aware of the boundaries that should not be crossed in the interests of camaraderie and fair play.

But this was just too good to pass up.

Even my partner, Ox, who normally wears the mantle of my protector, had contributed some shots of me in my undies at Maggie's apartment.

I was greeted with hoots and hollers and requests for a lap dance.

Finally, Captain Short called a halt to the pandemonium and with great difficulty restored a semblance of order.

With all the gravity he could muster, he addressed the packed squad room. "Gentlemen, I want to thank you all for a job well done. Through the efforts of our joint task force, another threat to our fine city has been thwarted. And we owe a special thanks to two of our very own, Officer George Wilson and his partner, Tina Williams."

The room exploded with another round of hoots and jeers.

I think I understood how Julius Caesar felt when Marc Anthony plunged the knife into his chest.

Then the captain raised his hand, and the room fell silent.

"I know many of you had your doubts when the City Retiree Action Patrol was formed, and I understand that. However, in reviewing the record for the past six months, I think it is clear that the Patrol has earned our acceptance and respect. These men, having given of themselves far beyond our expectations, have made an invaluable contribution in our quest for justice. I'm proud to serve with these fine officers. How about you?"

The room stood as one and applauded.

Okay, Captain, you're forgiven.

After Shorty had completed the daily assignments and the room had emptied, Ox, Vince, and I were the only ones remaining.

"In case you couldn't tell, I'm mighty proud of you three. You've done a fine job, but now you need a break. I have a special assignment for you."

I thought, *Oh great, every time the captain has a special assignment for us, I get to be gay or a john or a tranny. What next?*

"Don't look so skeptical. This will be fun."

"Exactly what is your definition of fun?" I asked.

"I'm sure you're aware that the economy is in the toilet this year. Stocks have tanked, property values have dropped, and unemployment is sky high. All of this has taken a toll on the Christmas charities. Every organization from the Salvation Army to the United Way is falling way behind. Christmas will be pretty bleak for a lot of families this year if they don't get a boost. The department wants to host a fund-raising event, and we would like for the three of you to put it together."

We all sat in stunned silence.

I looked at Ox and Vince. "Uh, Captain, none of us have ever put together a major event like that before."

"All you guys have to do is organize the pieces and make it happen. The big brass have already done the arm twisting. We have a banquet room in a big hotel, catering by a fancy restaurant, and the promise of lavish gifts for a silent auction. You fellows figure out what else you'll need and let me know. Oh, and we're also inviting the St. Sebastian's Children's Home, so we'll need a Santa Claus."

I took a look at Ox's two hundred and twenty pounds. "I don't think that will be a problem."

After the captain left, I turned to Vince. "You ever done anything like this before?"

165

"I've organized track meets and wrestling matches, but this is a whole new ballgame."

I looked at Ox, and he just shook his head.

"Okay, so we're going to need some help. Who are the experts at putting on a party?"

"Women!" we all shouted at once.

"You guys up for some pizza tonight?"

I picked up Maggie, Ox picked up Mary, and the rest of our merry little band gathered in my apartment.

After a round of meat lover's with extra cheese, we were ready to get to work. As I suspected, Maggie grabbed the bull by the horns and started handing out assignments like a drill sergeant.

When it was all said and done, Maggie, Mary, and Bernice would work with the caterers on the table decorations, food preparation, and serving line. The professor was our treasurer and would handle the silent auction and donations. Vince would work with the hotel staff in setting up the room, and Willie would collect the gifts for the "Toys For Tots" campaign. Ox would be occupied as Santa, and I was in charge of entertainment.

One solitary soul sat in our group without an assignment.

Maggie looked at me and winked, and I got the hint.

"Wow, entertainment for a huge crowd like that. Do any of you guys know a comedian that might be available that close to Christmas?"

Jerry lit up like a Christmas tree. "I think I know one who might be available."

We were all set to go.

After our planning session broke up, Vince pulled me aside.

"Walt, do you think we need to worry about security?"

With the economy in the tank, there had been a rash of burglaries of charitable institutions. Church collections for the needy had been taken, Salvation Army bell ringer pots had been stolen, and someone had even broken into a locked trailer and ripped off gifts for the "Toys For Tots" campaign.

"We are security. What kind of thief would try to rob an event sponsored by the police? There will be a hundred cops there that night."

"Yeah, I guess you're right."

The event was scheduled from 7:00 to 10:00 p.m., and as enthusiastic as Jerry was, I knew he didn't have enough material for a three-hour gig.

We needed a band.

As I've mentioned before, Maggie and I love to dance. We've taken ballroom classes and can do a pretty fair rumba, cha-cha, and fox trot, but our real love is old-time rock 'n' roll.

Our favorite band is, of course, The Krazy Kats.

Quite by accident, we heard them for the first time in a little club called *The Class Reunion*. The moment we heard them we were hooked.

While they are Kansas City-based, they play at American Legions, dance clubs, and casinos all over Missouri and Kansas. When Maggie and I started turning up at gigs in St. Joe, Columbia, and Overland Park, we soon came to be known as the "road warriors" and have been close friends ever since.

The thing you have to love about the Kats is that they have been playing together since 1957, and in 2007, Maggie and I were privileged to attend their fiftieth anniversary celebration.

Lee, Willie, and Fred can play any song from 50s, 60s and early 70s. They're approaching their seventieth birthdays, but to hear them play, you'd never know it. Lee can still hit that high note at the end of *Unchained Melody* as well as the Righteous Brothers ever could.

I gave Lee a call.

Before I could even tell him about the charity event, he wanted to know what was happening with the Elvis tapes.

Like me, he had been waiting impatiently for the announcement of this extraordinary discovery.

Also, like me, he was sworn to secrecy and couldn't even tell Willie and Fred, his closest friends.

I told him what I knew, which wasn't much, and assured him that the minute I heard anything, he'd be my first call.

Fortunately, they weren't booked that evening, and he readily agreed to perform for our charity event.

Our next chore was to find Ox a Santa outfit. We checked the yellow pages for costumes, made a list, and started making the rounds.

Since it was late in the season, many shops had sold out of Santa garb, but we finally found a place on Broadway that had one left.

As Ox stood in front of the mirror decked out in red flannel, white beard, and cap, he dropped the bomb on me.

"Walt, I'm going to do this on one condition."

"Condition! Where did that come from?"

"I'm not naïve. I've been to Macy's and seen the Santa there. He's got this cute little chick dressed in a short red skirt trimmed in white fluffy fur as his assistant. I want one of those."

"Yeah, I'll bet you do. Maybe we can switch Mary from the serving table. I bet she'd look great in a fur-lined tutu."

"If she takes off seventy pounds and fifty years, you've got a deal."

The sales clerk overhearing our conversation stepped right in. "Let me help you out here. I don't have any more Santa's Helper skirts, but I do have one elf suit left."

"Elf suit? Why in the world would we want an— Oh no!"

169

"Perfect!" Ox replied. "We'll take it."

"Why me?" I moaned.

"Hey, if I have to dress up like Santa, I'll need a helper, and you're my partner. Right? Besides, you'll be really cute in your pointy little hat and shoes."

Finally, the big night arrived, and with Maggie cracking the whip, everything seemed to be in place.

Arriving guests were greeted by a receiving line composed of the department's top brass and were immediately escorted to the tables loaded with silent auction gifts under the watchful eye of the professor.

Our caterer had provided a scrumptious array of munchies: little weenies in barbecue sauce, cheese and crackers, fruit, and tiny meatballs in some kind of gravy. You know how I feel about gravy.

In the far corner of the room, a stage and dance floor had been erected.

Since the crowd would be coming and going throughout the evening, we decided to alternate Jerry's stand-up routine with The Krazy Kats. Each would perform twice.

Jerry took the stage with a scattering of polite applause and grabbed the mike.

"Two young boys were spending the night at their grandparents the week before Christmas. At bedtime,

170

the two boys knelt beside their beds to say their prayers when the youngest one began praying at the top of his lungs, 'I pray for a new bicycle; I pray for a new X-Box; I pray for more Legos.'

"His older brother leaned over and nudged the younger brother and said, 'Why are you shouting your prayers? God isn't deaf.' To which the little brother replied, 'No, but Grandma is!'"

The crowd roared with laughter. Jerry never missed a beat.

"A lady was picking through the frozen turkeys at the grocery store but couldn't find one big enough for her family for Christmas dinner. She asked the stock boy, 'Do these turkeys get any bigger?'

"The stock boy replied, 'No, ma'am, they're dead.'"

Another round of laughter. Jerry had them hooked.

As Jerry was regaling the adults, Ox and I were in another corner dressed as Santa and his elf. A large department store had donated a North Pole setup consisting of a gingerbread house, a large ornate chair for Santa, and a pathway lined with six-foot plastic candy canes to channel the waiting tots to the fat man.

I had made Ox promise not to tell a soul about my elfdom, but, as usual, word had leaked and spread throughout the precinct.

Everyone had to stroll by and take a shot.

"Who sings *Blue Christmas* and makes toy guitars? Elfis."

"What do you call a transvestite elf? Walt."

The kids from the St. Sebastian Children's Home arrived and queued up in line to share their Christmas wishes with Santa.

We hoped the first kid to sit on Santa's lap wasn't a harbinger of things to come. He leaned over, gave Santa a sniff, and proclaimed, "You smell like moth balls."

Mostly, things went well until a gorgeous little girl with blonde hair and blue eyes whispered in Ox's ear, "Can you bring my mommy and daddy back? That's all I really want."

I think maybe a tear slid down into Santa's beard.

After Jerry's first act, The Krazy Kats took the stage and captured the audience with their rendition of *Old Time Rock and Roll.* Their set was, of course, all the good stuff from the 50s. The crowd loved it when Willie, the keyboard player, broke into his version of *Great Balls of Fire* and played with his nose and elbows.

It's the Kats' tradition to end the first set with Lee's Elvis impersonation. Actually, it's more of a parody than an impersonation. He curls his lip, wiggles his leg, does a few karate kicks, and belts out a half dozen Elvis hits. His fans love it.

By break time, all the kids had visited Santa, and Ox and I thankfully swapped our costumes for our civvies. We were just finishing when Lee came into the bathroom to change out of his Elvis jumpsuit.

"Lee, that was great. Thank you so much."

"No problem. You know we love to play, especially for a good cause. By the way, are you coming to the big Elvis birthday party?"

Elvis Presley's birthday is January eighth, and every year Kansas City Elvis fans have a celebration. I had been so busy with my undercover operation I hadn't given it a thought.

"I'm sure I'll try. You know how much I love Elvis. Anything special this year?"

"Well, yeah. It's his seventy-fifth birthday. They're really doing it up big. Big names are coming from all over the country, and they've invited The Krazy Kats to perform. Wouldn't it be great if the new recordings were ready by then?"

"It certainly would, but I wouldn't get my hopes up. Either way, I wouldn't miss it."

I had no idea how prophetic that would be.

The gala event came to a close. Kids had shared their Christmas dreams with Santa. Adults had eaten, danced, laughed, and pledged thousands of dollars for the various charities, and the professor's cash box was overflowing with the receipts from the silent auction.

Now it was cleanup time. Somehow it's not near as much fun tearing down as it is setting up.

The band had packed up and left, Maggie and the girls were clearing the food table, Willie was stacking chairs on a four-wheeled dolly, and Ox and I were tearing down Santa's Castle.

Vince, whose job had been to liaison with the hotel maintenance staff, was in a dither because the workers had not made an appearance since the festivities ended, leaving the cleanup to us volunteers.

"They're probably in the maintenance room hiding out until we get most of the work done. I'll go see if I can smoke 'em out."

No sooner had Vince left through one door than three guys in gray jumpsuits with brooms, mops, and trash cans appeared through a different door. They busied themselves sweeping and picking up trash as they worked their way toward the silent auction table.

Then, on cue, they dropped their brooms and mops, pulled ski masks and revolvers from their jumpsuits, and started giving orders.

"Okay, old timers, just do as you're told and nobody gets hurt."

Turning to the professor, one said, "Hand over the cash box, Grandpa, and do it quick."

The professor had just passed the precious box to the masked man when Vince reentered the room.

"Hey, guys! I found the maintenance men tied up in the—What the hell? What's going on here?"

The guy with the cash box turned and fired a volley at Vince and yelled, "Okay, let's split." The thieves took off in different directions.

One was approaching the serving line.

I saw Maggie grab a chafing dish with remnants of the meatballs and gravy and fling pan and all into the path of the oncoming thief. The pan exploded on the floor, and greasy gravy spread like flowing lava. The thief saw it too late, and as he entered the gravy swamp, his feet flew out from under him, and he landed flat on his back.

Not to be left out of the action, Mary had grabbed her weapon of choice, a baseball bat, from the "Toys For Tots" collection and rushed to the fallen thief.

"We worked hard for this money, and I'll be damned if I'm gonna let some peckerhead take it from us. Now go ahead. Just give me a reason to use this."

Vince was in pursuit of the guy who had taken a shot at him. He had to move cautiously as the fleeing felon repeatedly turned to fire.

His path was taking him past the area where Willie had been folding chairs. Upon hearing gunfire, Willie had crouched among the chairs and saw the thief coming his way running full tilt.

Just as the masked man turned and looked back to fire another round at Vince, Willie pushed the dolly loaded with chairs into the aisle.

The thief hit the dolly at a dead run and was knocked out cold.

Vince was on him in a flash and cuffed him. Getting to his feet, he and Willie bumped chests and did a high-five.

Teamwork.

The third thief was headed in our direction.

Ox and I were buried in the bowels of Santa's gingerbread house when the first shots were fired. I saw that he would pass by our candy cane lane, and seeing the six-foot striped poles gave me an idea.

When I was a kid visiting my grandparents' farm, Grandma would tell me to go to the chicken yard and bring her a hen. I had a wire about four feet long with a hook at the end. I would select my victim and chase the poor thing around the yard until I got close enough to hook it around the ankle. Grandpa would dispatch the hen with an axe, and before the day was over, we had fried chicken on the table.

I grabbed a candy cane, and as the thief sped by the gingerbread house, I snagged his foot, and he came crashing down.

I never cease to wonder at the twists and turns in our life's journey.

Who could ever predict that the chicken-catching adventures of a six-year-old kid would someday morph into the thief-catching adventures of a sixty-six-year-old cop?

After the charity thieves were hauled away and my little band had gathered to rehash the evening's events, I couldn't help but think about another Christmas long ago.

A Man was born into the world to bring hope to the poor and suffering.

Kings came from afar to bring gifts to glorify Him. Tonight, people had poured out their hearts and their wallets to help these same poor and suffering souls, but men of ill will tried to take it away.

The day was saved not by kings or royalty but by plain, ordinary folks who care.

I'll bet Lady Justice and the Big Guy are smiling.

CHAPTER 12

We had pulled a double-whammy.

The charity event was a huge success. Thousands of dollars had been raised, and a truck full of toys was ready for delivery to deserving children.

The bonus was the capture of the charity thieves. All in all, it was an evening well spent.

The captain had intended that this be a cushy, stress-free assignment to give us a break from murder, mayhem, and thievery, but since it didn't turn out exactly like that, he insisted we take a few days of well-deserved rest.

I was looking forward to a peaceful celebration of the Christmas/New Year holidays, and I was especially excited about the upcoming commemoration of Elvis's seventy-fifth birthday.

I had slept late and had just poured myself a cup of coffee when I noticed the headline in the Kansas City Star. The headline in bold print announced, *"Lost Elvis Tapes Discovered By Local Pastor."*

This was the announcement I had been waiting for.

The front-page story recounted the life of the musical Johnson family and confirmed my suspicions as to the origin of the tapes. It went on to say that a deal had been struck with RCA Records, which had produced most of Elvis's original recordings, and that they were working diligently to get the new release into the hands of Elvis's adoring fans.

The company in charge of publicity had decided that since the tapes were found in Kansas City and were most likely recorded by a Kansas City jazz musician, the new album should debut in Kansas City as well. Wanting to squeeze as much coverage as possible out of the event, RCA had decided to sponsor the annual Elvis impersonation contest that usually accompanies his birthday celebration. They sweetened the deal by saying that the winner of the contest would perform live on the night of the album's debut and be awarded a $25,000 prize.

Local clubs and bars were sponsoring mini-contests where Elvis wannabes would compete, and the winner would represent that club or bar at the next level of competition.

Elvis was everywhere!

Now that the story was out, I was free to share my involvement with Maggie, Ox, Vince, and anyone else who would listen.

I called Lee, but he was way ahead of me and was as excited as a kid on Christmas morning.

After sharing the news with my own little circle of friends, I achieved a certain celebrity status.

Maggie loves Elvis almost as much as I do, and we vowed to make the most of this once-in-a-lifetime opportunity. Almost every night we went to a different bar and watched the impersonators compete for the chance to be part of music history.

It was kind of like watching the American Idol auditions: there were a few good ones, but most were a dismal failure.

This year they had introduced a new twist to the competition: they had separate singing and lip-sync competitions.

You have to understand that Elvis was the complete package. He had the looks, the moves, and a voice that God gives to very few mortal men.

No one else has it all.

There are guys who can sing almost as well, but the voice is in a body that isn't even close. There are guys who have the looks but can't sing a note, but there are hardly any who have the onstage presence, demeanor, and moves that to the King were the natural expression of his music.

The new competition opened the field to a whole new body of Elvis fans whose dream was to pay tribute to their idol.

Kansas City, Missouri, was in the national spotlight. As the day for the debut of the new album drew closer, Elvis fans flooded the city. Soon there wasn't a hotel room to be found anywhere within thirty miles of the city.

The event was to be in the new Sprint Center Arena, and the nineteen thousand seats were sold out on the first day. And, of course, the police department had their hands full as rowdy partygoers and revelers filled the nightclubs and bars.

But even more bizarre was the crime that seemed to be focused on the impersonator competitions. Fistfights would erupt between competitors, and threats of bodily harm were reported to police.

One evening, Maggie and I attended a competition where the representatives of four bars from the Westport area vied for the opportunity to represent Westport in the next stage of the contest. All four were pretty decent, but one guy was clearly the best and was finally declared the winner.

The next morning at squad meeting, the captain announced that the guy who had won the Westport contest was dragged from his car into an alley and so severely beaten that he would be unable to continue the competition.

After the rest of the squad was dismissed, the captain asked Ox and I to stay.

"We've got a real problem on our hands. The whole nation—heck, the whole world is focused on Kansas City right now, and people are getting mugged all over the place. So much attention is directed toward these contests, and now we're getting winners almost beaten to death. It's bad publicity, and the city fathers are having a conniption fit. They want it stopped. It's bad for business. There's a lot of shit hitting the fan at City Hall, and you know the old saying, 'Shit runs downhill.'"

I didn't like where this was going.

"What exactly do you need from us?" I asked.

"Walt, we need your help. We need you undercover."

"Undercover as what?"

"As an Elvis impersonator."

"No. No! I can't do this! You had me as an undercover john at a strip club because I looked old and needy. Then you had me in a gay bar because Vince and I made a great couple. Then I had to be a transvestite because I was the only cop who could look good in a dress. What in heaven's name makes you think I can be an Elvis impersonator?"

"Calm down, Walt. Just think about it. There's no bigger Elvis fan than you. You've been listening to his music for fifty years and know every one of his songs by heart. You and Maggie are great dancers, so I know you've got some moves. Most of our guys can't put one foot in front of the other without tripping. You're all we've got!"

"But I'm sixty-six years old."

"So what? Isn't Elvis seventy-five this year?"

He had me there.

I sighed. "What's the plan?"

"Since the winner of the Westport contest can't continue, they're going to hold it again in a week. You will be the new entry to replace the guy who got mugged. We've made arrangements for Ox to be a bouncer at the club, and we'll have backup close by. If the mugger makes a move on the next winner, we'll be ready."

"In a week? You expect me to transform into Elvis in a week?"

"Oh, come on, Walt. We don't expect you to win. You just need to be there. I know you've seen some of these guys perform, and most are pretty crappy. I'm sure you'll fit right in."

"Gee, thanks for the vote of confidence."

So how do you go about making a sixty-six-year-old guy look like Elvis Presley?

You start with a costume.

There are three distinct Elvis personas that impersonators use in their acts: the young, sleek Elvis with slicked back pompadour and duck-tails, circa 1955 to 1966; the more mature Elvis dressed in the black leather outfit from the 1968 Comeback Special; and the Elvis of the concert tour years with the flashy, studded jumpsuits.

I knew without a doubt that I couldn't pull off the early stuff, so I was off to find a jumpsuit.

Ox and I had just recently patronized multiple costume shops in search of a Santa outfit, so we knew exactly where to go. The first shop had a pretty good selection of suits. Elvis had dozens that he used on his concert tours. I had seen many of them at Graceland in the museum.

I tried on a black one. It made me look like an old ninja. The red one made me think of my grandpa in his pair of red long johns.

Then I saw it.

It was pure white with a beautiful design made of multicolored glass studs and a full billowing cape with the same design. It was perfect.

The shopkeeper said I could rent the suit, but we would have to buy a wig. I guess that's a good thing.

He only had one Elvis style wig. I tried it on, and it made me look like Don King.

On the way home, I stopped by my barbershop, plopped into the chair, and donned my unruly hairpiece.

"Mac, is there anything you can do with this?"

He just grinned. I guess he'd seen it all, hair-wise, at one time or another.

"Sure, let's give it a try."

When he was finished, I didn't look like Don King anymore, more of a cross between Roy Orbison, Neil Diamond, and Elvis. But it would have to do.

I had called Maggie and asked her to meet me at my apartment. I was hoping she could perform some makeup magic that would take about twenty years off my appearance.

After her initial shock at my announcement, she insisted on seeing me in full costume. Once her fits of laughter had passed, she surveyed my predicament with a more critical eye.

"With all your wrinkles, you look like Mick Jagger. We've got to do something with that hair."

"It's all Mac's fault."

She got her scissors, brush, and can of hairspray, and in fifteen minutes she held up a mirror.

It actually almost looked like Elvis's hair.

183

"Now about the wrinkles," I said.

"I'm afraid that's a lost cause. I'm Maggie, not the Virgin Mary. I can't perform miracles."

How comforting.

"Sit still. I've got an idea."

I heard her rummaging around in one of my dresser drawers, and she returned with a huge pair of sunglasses.

"Here, this will hide most of your face."

"Elvis didn't wear sunglasses on stage."

"Maybe not, but I think this Elvis should."

I slipped them on and stood in front of my full-length mirror.

I was prepared to be appalled at my appearance, but as I gazed at my reflection, something stirred inside of me that I had never felt before.

The dread that I had been experiencing since my meeting with the captain was replaced, at least for a fleeting moment, by a feeling of empowerment.

In that brief moment, I saw not the old fart dressed in a costume, but the King, ready to pour his heart out for his fans.

My feeling of euphoria quickly vanished at the thought of getting on stage in front of hundreds of people.

What was I going to perform?

I went to my video library and pulled out my two favorite concerts: *Aloha From Hawaii* and *That's The Way It Is* from the Las Vegas International Hotel.

Maggie and I watched, enthralled, as the King performed his magic.

I had seen these dozens of times, but this time was different. I tried to memorize his stance, his hand gestures, and the way his body moved with the rhythm of the music.

After the videos, Maggie had to leave. She had early appointments the next day. I went to bed, but my mind wouldn't shut down.

In my real estate days, I had attended many seminars given by top-selling agents. One of their mantras was "If you can imagine it, you can achieve it." I had spent many hours imagining myself in front of buyer and seller clients, saying the right words to help them make a decision.

This night I lay there imagining myself on stage mimicking the persona of my idol.

I didn't sleep much.

I did, however, choose the song I would perform: *Jailhouse Rock.*

The next morning, I put *Jailhouse Rock* in my CD player and stood in front of my full-length mirror.

What kid hasn't pretended to be a rock star like Tom Cruise in *Risky Business*? I know I did.

I tried to put my body into motion the way I had imagined it the night before, but it just didn't look right. After an hour of frustration, I was ready to give up. Who was I kidding? Me? Elvis? Get real!

Then I remembered the fleeting moment when I had first seen myself as Elvis, and I put on my outfit. I went back to the mirror, and that feeling of empowerment filled me again. I turned on the music and let it rip.

What is it about capes and costumes? Almost every superhero finds previously unknown abilities in the anonymity of their disguise. Look at Superman or Batman. The moves that looked so stupid a few short minutes before in my pajamas really looked pretty good in my jeweled jumpsuit.

I practiced for an hour and was almost satisfied with my performance, but something still wasn't quite right.

Then it hit me. It was the hands. I needed something in my hands, a mike or maybe a guitar.

I remembered that I had seen an old acoustic guitar in the corner of Willie's apartment. I gave him a call and asked him to bring it up.

The look on Willie's face when I opened the door and he was face to face with Elvis was priceless.

I spent the next hour calming him down and giving him the details of my undercover operation. I swore him to secrecy, and he promised he wouldn't blow my cover. He also promised that he was going to be in the audience for my big debut.

Swell.

Back in front of the mirror with my new prop in hand, I went through the routine again.

It worked. It was the final piece of the puzzle.

I spent the rest of the day smoothing the rough edges. I lip-synced *Jailhouse Rock* so many times I could probably sing it backwards. By nightfall, I was comfortable with my performance. Surprisingly, my feeling of dread had turned into excitement and anticipation.

I was ready.

I think it was probably a good thing that the contest was taking place right away. It didn't give me a lot of time to stew around and let my self-doubts creep back in.

Plus, we had the details of the undercover operation to iron out. Ox would be on-site posing as a bouncer, and another squad car was parked in front of a donut shop a block away.

I had my trusty mike wire taped to my chest so I could communicate with Ox and the backup car. I had been given an alias, Mike Morgan, to protect my undercover identity.

The M.O. of the attacker was to hit the winner of the contest and inflict enough damage to take him out of the competition.

Someone really wanted to win.

Maggie and I arrived at the club at 7:00 p.m. The contest was scheduled to begin at eight. The house was packed, standing room only, and a long line was queued on the sidewalk in front of the building. Ox had been on duty since five.

We were escorted to a dressing room, and Maggie helped transform me from mild-mannered cop to rock star.

Not an easy task.

We drew straws to determine the order in which we would perform. Of course I got the short straw and would go on last. I really wanted to get it over with.

As I stood in the wing waiting my turn, I broke out in a sweat, and my tummy was attacked by a swarm of butterflies. No, I think it was more like a pack of vultures.

What in heaven's name am I doing here?

Then I remembered seeing footage of Elvis backstage as his introduction was playing, and I remembered a candid interview where he confessed to being scared to death before each and every performance. His fear was not of performing but of disappointing his fans. He always wanted to give his best.

I wasn't really scared of performing. Every time Maggie and I are the first or sometimes the only dancers on the floor, it's a performance. All eyes in the room are on us, and it's okay because we're comfortable with what we do.

The only difference here was my confidence in what I was about to do.

I closed my eyes and visualized Elvis on stage and rehearsed in my mind the performance I had practiced for hours.

I was shaken from my reverie by the booming voice of the announcer. "Please welcome our final contestant in the Westport Elvis competition."

A roar went up from the audience, not for me, but for the legend I was portraying.

I strode onto the stage, guitar slung on my shoulder, and with all the Elvis I could muster pointed to the sound technician. "Hit it, Scotty."

As *Jailhouse Rock* blasted from the speakers, my body kicked into gear, and for the next three minutes, I was the King.

The announcer assembled all four of us on the stage. The rules were fairly simple: he would stand behind each contestant, and the audience would cheer for their favorite. An applause meter would record each response and determine the winner.

Each contestant received enthusiastic applause, but when he held his hand over my head, a thunderous cheer erupted from the crowd.

"I don't think we even have to look at the meter. The clear winner is contestant number four, Mike Morgan."

I stood there dumbfounded.

I looked out into the audience and saw my old friend Willie clapping and smiling so wide his gold tooth glistened in the spotlights.

In the post-performance interview, I shared my cover story as a sixty-six-year-old retired realtor (which was partly true), and they immediately determined I was by far the oldest contestant in the citywide competition.

The story in the Kansas City Star the next morning had dubbed me 'Grandpa Elvis.'

Swell.

I had made arrangements for Vince to pick up Maggie and take her home. If the mugger struck, I didn't want her anywhere near the action.

I changed from my jumpsuit to my civvies and hung around the dressing room until things quieted down in the club.

I tapped my mike and announced to Ox and the backup car that I would be leaving the club through the back exit. We wanted to give the perp every opportunity to make his move.

I waited a few minutes to give Ox time to get into position and left the building. As I crossed the dark alley to the parking lot, I glanced around, fully expecting an attacker to emerge from the black shadows.

I reached my parked car without incident and made a point of fussing around in the trunk and backseat to give the perp another opportunity to strike.

Nothing.

After a few minutes, Ox came around the building. "Hey, Walt, it doesn't look like he's going to show. Let's pack it in for tonight."

We were disappointed that our elaborate plan didn't lure the mugger into the open, but we would get another chance.

After all, I had won.

I drove home and wearily climbed the stairs to my apartment. I hadn't realized how much the evening had taken out of me. I had been riding an adrenaline high, but now that it had subsided, I was pooped.

I opened the door and was surprised to find Maggie in the living room. Vince was supposed to take her home.

She greeted me with a big hug and kiss.

"Hey, *Tiger Man.* you did some *Good Rockin Tonight.*"

Maggie knows her Elvis songs.

"I saw you on that stage and thought, *You're The Devil In Disguise.* It kinda turned me on, and I thought that maybe *Tonight Is So Right For Love.*"

"Oh, Maggie, I'm beat. I'm afraid that's just *Too Much Monkey Business.*"

"But Walt, I've got this *Burning Love.* You'll be sorry."

"Maggie, you're a *Hard Headed Woman. Don't Be Cruel.*"

"Come on, big boy, *Treat Me Nice.*"

"Oh, Maggie, *I Beg Of You.*"

Then her playfulness turned to tenderness. "Walt, *Have I Told You Lately That I Love You?*"

Knowing I was defeated, I replied, "Okay, you can have me *Anyway You Want Me.*"

"*Just Love Me Tender.*"

And I did.

CHAPTER 13

Since most of my undercover work had lent itself to the slings and arrows of my fellow officers, I expected a raucous greeting as I entered the station.

I wasn't disappointed.

In addition to the usual hoots and hollers, a few guys asked for my autograph, and a meter maid threw a pair of lace panties at me.

The price of fame.

The mood changed quickly as a grim-faced captain entered the room.

"Last night the winner of the Power and Light District's contest was out celebrating with friends. Their party broke up about 1:00 a.m., and the winner was accosted in his home driveway. He has a broken leg.

"Looks like we were in the wrong place and the wrong time. The mugger's previous M.O. had been to attack the winner shortly after a victory, but he apparently changed his routine to throw us off track, and it worked.

"We'll have no choice but to put a tail on each of the contest winners. We have no idea where he will strike next.

"At least we still have our foot in the door since 'Grandpa Elvis' was victorious in Westport last night."

Another outburst of bawdy laughter filled the room.

I guess my mission in life is to provide the comic relief for our squad.

"The semifinals are tomorrow night. They've changed the venue to Kemper Arena to accommodate more fans. It will be a busy evening. There are twelve entries, six contestants in each category, and eight will be eliminated, leaving a total of four contestants to protect until the finals. We'll have our hands full. With the huge crowd, there will naturally be police everywhere, so we don't think he will make a move at Kemper.

"Two officers will be protecting each contestant. Your assignments are on the duty board. Ox and Vince will be with Walt.

"Good luck, men. Stay on your toes."

As I hurried from the squad room, Dooley shouted after me, "Hey, Grandpa, break a leg."

Show business.

I was anxious to get home and practice. In the semifinals, each contestant would do two songs, so I had to work up a second number, but something was nagging at me.

Every crime has a motive. The obvious motive here was the $25,000 prize and the opportunity to perform at the history-making debut of the lost Elvis tapes. The winner would be the subject of music lore for years, and it could possibly be the jump-start of a new career.

If this were indeed the motive, the obvious suspects would be the finalists themselves. Someone was eliminating the competition.

I stopped by Captain Short's office and asked if he had a list of the finalists. I shared my theory with him and wasn't really surprised when he said that the brass were way ahead of me.

Assigning officers to guard the contestants was to be expected. The bonus would be the opportunity to keep an eye on them for suspicious activity.

He copied the list, and I headed home for rehearsal. The song I chose for my second number was *Heartbreak Hotel.* I donned my jumpsuit, flipped on the CD player, and visualized Elvis belting out his classic hit.

What I discovered was that learning moves to a song wasn't unlike learning a new dance step.

Maggie and I had taken dozens of dance lessons, and when the instructor introduced a new step, we would often struggle for hours with the timing and footwork. But if we kept at it, everything would eventually fall into place. After we finally got it, we would practice the step and incorporate it into our normal routine, and somehow it got hardwired into our bodies. After that, the movements came naturally.

I stayed in front of the mirror and repeated the song over and over until I didn't even have to think about it.

I was ready.

After hours of exhausting practice, I sat down with a glass of Arbor Mist and pulled out the list of contestants. The department had put together a very detailed account of each man's life. After all, they were suspects. I had seen several of them perform in the clubs before I was drafted, but I hadn't seen them all.

As I read through the list, it was quite obvious that the younger set dominated the competition. Ten of the contestants were between eighteen and thirty. One guy was forty-five, and I came crippling along at sixty-six.

The only mature jumpsuit Elvis's were two old guys. It would be interesting to see if age and experience would win out over youthful exuberance.

Kemper Arena was packed.

All 19,500 seats had been sold, and a screen had been set up outside the arena for fans that couldn't get a ticket.

Maggie and I arrived an hour before show time and were escorted into the bowels of the huge arena to a small underground wing housing a series of small, private dressing rooms.

The wing had massive heavy doors that could be locked tight for security purposes. Over the years, celebrities and rock stars had performed at the

Kemper, and this heavily guarded sanctuary was designed to insulate the idols from their adoring fans.

Maggie did her magic once again and transformed the old fart into a rock star as best she could. My advantage at the Kemper was that I was farther away from the audience than I was at the intimate club. My wrinkles and waddle were harder to detect from a distance.

I was to perform in the tenth slot, so I settled in for a long wait.

Maggie took her seat in the audience, and I sat in silence, rehearsing each move over and over.

Finally, there was a knock on the door. "Five minutes, Mr. Morgan."

And of course the buzzards returned in full force. I was led through the labyrinth of halls to a stairway that opened into a backstage holding area. Contestant number nine was just finishing his act, and I peeked around a curtain onto the arena stage.

"Holy crap!"

I had been to the Kemper and Sprint Center before, usually sitting somewhere in the nosebleed section, and it was always an awesome experience.

But there was no way I could ever imagine the impact and thrill of actually being on the stage, bathed in spotlights, with 19,000 screaming fans cheering me on.

There is no doubt in my mind that everyone at some time in their life imagines themselves in the spotlight as a singer, dancer, musician, or poet, but few actually get to live it.

It was awesome!

Then I heard the announcer's booming voice. "Please welcome contestant number ten representing Westport, Mr. Mike Morgan, 'Grandpa Elvis.'"

I strode onto the stage, and thank goodness I had practiced until my performance was automatic because my brain was on overload.

I queued the technician, and as *Jailhouse Rock* boomed through the auditorium, my body kicked into gear.

I have to admit, in retrospect, I can't really remember what I did. It all just happened, but I still vividly remember the thunderous applause as I bowed and left the stage.

A stagehand guided me back through the hallway maze to my dressing room, and I closed the door. I collapsed into a chair in a daze, my mind still reeling from the impact of that amazing experience.

After about fifteen minutes, I started coming down from my adrenaline-induced high and changed into my civvies. I was finished for the evening.

As each ticket holder took their seats, they were given a ballot with twelve entrants. They were to circle their four favorites and turn the ballot in as they exited the building. The four contestants with the highest number of votes would be the four finalists.

I heard the last contestant being led down the hall, and I gathered my things and started for the door.

But it wouldn't open.

I struggled with the knob and pulled and tugged, but it wouldn't budge.

Irritated, I banged on the door with my fist.

"Hey, is anyone out there? I need some help with this door."

Then I smelled it and saw it at the same time. Smoke was billowing in from under the door.

In a panic, I struggled and pulled at the knob with more intensity, but it didn't move.

I yelled again but received no reply.

By this time the smoke was rising to head level, and I began to cough.

I looked frantically around the room for another avenue of escape, but there was none. Being in the bowels of the arena, there were, of course, no windows.

Remembering a lesson from my Boy Scout training, I found a rag and soaked it with water and tied it around my face. It helped, but I could see the room filling fast.

I had to find a way out.

Then I saw it: a vent in the corner of the ceiling, probably a heating and cooling duct.

I pulled a chair into the corner and climbed up for a closer look. Warm, pure air was flowing out of the vent but fighting a losing battle against the rising smoke. I looked for the screws that held the vent in place, and thankfully they were slotted and not Phillips. I fished around in my pocket and found a dime. It wasn't much of a screwdriver, but it would have to do.

The smoke had now reached ceiling level, and I prayed that the screws weren't rusted shut.

Thankfully, the four screws backed out easily, and the vent cover fell to the floor.

I peered inside. The duct was about eighteen inches square, barely enough room to squeeze my 145-pound body through.

Ox would have never made it.

I boosted myself into the duct and gulped a lungful of the clean air.

I had never experienced claustrophobia, but then I'd never tried to wriggle through a tunnel that touched me on all four sides.

I remembered reading Thor Heyerdahl's Kon Tiki and his experience in the underground tunnels of Easter Island.

If he could do it, so could I.

I inched my way along the duct for about twenty feet and came to another vent that opened not into another room but into the hallway.

I saw a figure coming my way and was about to cry out for help when I saw him bend down in front of a dressing room door and add fuel to the fire burning there.

It was the perp.

I couldn't see who it was because his face was covered with a breathing device of some kind.

I watched as he went from door to door, adding fuel at each one. If each dressing room were like the one I just left, the other contestants would soon succumb to the smoke.

I had to do something quickly.

I saw him round a corner and disappear into the next hallway.

I examined the hallway vent. The screw heads were on the outside, so I would have to break out from the inside.

Due to the restricting confines of the duct, my arms were stretched out in front of me, and I had difficulty getting into a position where I could apply pressure to the vent. I was finally in place. I hoped the screws were not tapped into metal. If they were, I was sunk. I hit the vent with all the leverage I could muster, the screws popped out of the brittle drywall, and I was free.

Well, sort of.

I looked out of the vent opening and saw the floor about ten feet below. In my present position, I could wiggle out head first, but I wasn't sure I could survive the ten-foot drop. My other option was to inch my way past the opening, contort my body so that my feet went out first, then roll onto my stomach and drop.

My sixty-six-year-old body wasn't thrilled with either option, but the latter seemed to offer the best chance of survival.

I twisted and turned and finally was poised with my ass end hanging out of the vent. I took a deep breath and launched myself into the hallway.

As I hit the floor, I remembered an old joke about a fall not being dangerous; it's the sudden stop at the end that gets you.

They were right.

I lay stunned in the smoke-filled hallway but hurriedly pulled myself together as I heard the perp's foot-steps coming my way.

I retreated down the hall in the opposite direction frantically looking for something to defend myself with.

I spotted a glass enclosure set into the hallway wall next to a bathroom door.

A fire extinguisher.

I grabbed the extinguisher and ducked into the bathroom just as the perp came around the corner. I hurriedly read the directions on the canister and pulled the pin as directed.

I cracked the door an inch, and as the perp walked by, I burst from the bathroom.

"Hold it right there, buster!"

When the perp turned to face me, I squeezed the handle, and a wave of foam blasted him square in the face.

He staggered back, momentarily blinded, and I whacked him on the head with the canister.

Seeing he was out cold, I raced along the hallway, spraying foam on the fires in front of each door. Then I retraced my steps, opening each door he had secured from the outside, and ten coughing contestants poured into the hallway.

Ten!

Someone was missing. Then it dawned on me.

I returned to the fallen perp and removed the breathing mask. The forty-five-year-old Elvis lay unconscious on the floor.

We made our way to the massive double doors that sealed the wing from the rest of the arena, threw them open, and gulped lungfuls of fresh air.

Police, Kemper security guards, and firemen flooded the hallway.

I saw a blur coming at me. It was Maggie.

She didn't say a word. She just buried her tear-stained face in my neck and held me tight.

The perp's name was John Martin.

He had spent his entire life as a second-banana entertainer but had finally gotten his big break in Branson, Missouri. For many seasons, he had been the Elvis impersonator in the *"Legends in Concert"* theater show, but the years had not been kind to John.

The late night hours, rich food, and booze had taken their toll.

The 'Legends' theater owners, seeing their attendance dwindle, opted to make a change to a young, vibrant Elvis, and John was put out to pasture.

The employment prospects for a forty-five-year-old washed-up Elvis impersonator are pretty slim.

John saw this contest and the resurgence in Elvis's popularity brought on by the lost tapes as his last hope for fame and fortune.

With his twisted logic, he thought he could improve his chances of winning by eliminating the competition.

Desperation can drive a man to unthinkable deeds.

CHAPTER 14

Once the door to freedom was opened at Kemper, all of us contestants were fitted with oxygen masks and whisked off to the hospital. After exhausting physicals, we were released. Thankfully, no one was seriously injured.

Maggie drove me home, and I stumbled into bed. It was almost noon when I awakened. My head ached, and my body felt like it had been run over by an eighteen-wheeler.

My breakfast was black coffee and aspirin. I sat in my easy chair, nursing my coffee and my pain, gazing out the front window.

I don't know how long I sat there, but during that time, I saw each of my friends, Willie, the professor, Jerry, and Bernice leave the building and return.

Each was alone.

I looked around at the familiar surroundings of my comfortable apartment. I had been happy there.

But something was missing.

Each time I tried to move, my old body reminded me of the trauma I had subjected it to, and it occurred to me that I had almost gotten my ticket punched three times in the last month.

I was alone. I hurt. I felt sorry for myself. The phone rang, jolting me out of my reverie.

"Walt, this is Shorty. How are you doing today?"

"I've had better days, but I'll live."

"In all the confusion last night, we didn't have much of a chance to talk. On behalf of the department, the contestants, and Kemper Arena, I want to thank you for a job well done. Have you seen this morning's paper?"

"Nope. I haven't moved around much yet."

"Well, get ready for your fifteen minutes of fame. The headline reads, *'Grandpa Elvis Saves The Day!'*"

"Swell. Just what I need."

"And if that's not enough to cheer you up—"

"What?"

"You won! You're a finalist in the Elvis competition."

I didn't know whether to laugh or cry.

"You're thirty-three years older than the next oldest contestant, and the fans are amazed that an old guy can move like you do. Plus, you're the only contestant that was actually alive the same time as Elvis, a contemporary, so to speak."

"So what now?"

"So now you get ready for the final next week. Since the mugger was caught, we figured we didn't need you undercover anymore. We explained the operation to the press and gave them your real name. 'Grandpa Elvis' is now Walt Williams. We know you'll make us proud.

"By the way, each contestant will be doing a four-song set, so take the rest of the week off. Break a leg!"

Great. Now I'll have two broken legs.

After the captain signed off, I just sat there staring into space.

Me? In the Sprint Center arena? Doing a four-number set in front of 19,000 people? On the same night that the lost Elvis tapes are revealed to the world?

Holy cow!

I picked up the phone and dialed. "Maggie, I—"

"Oh, I know! I'm so excited. I can hardly wait."

"Maggie, I need you."

She promised to come over as soon as she finished some paperwork.

I put on my Elvis videos hoping for inspiration for my two additional numbers.

Elvis had just finished gyrating through *Polk Salad Annie* when the phone rang again.

I figured it was Ox or Vince or one of the guys who had read the paper and was calling to give me a hard time.

I wish it had been.

The words I heard left me numb.

"Walt, this is Brother Hank. They've got Gracie!"

Forgetting about my aches and pains, I threw on my clothes and headed for Brother Hank's parsonage. I called Maggie and told her not to come over. I said I'd explain later.

Brother Hank met me at the door with red, swollen eyes and trembling hands.

"Okay, Brother Hank. Start from the beginning and tell me everything."

"Gracie went out to walk the dog. When she didn't return right away, I went to look for her. The dog was leashed to the mailbox, and this note was attached to her collar."

I looked at the note. It read, "If you ever want to see your wife alive again, you'll give us the tapes. Stay by the phone. We'll be in touch."

"Does anyone else know about this?"

"No, Walt. I called you first. I figured you'd know what to do."

"This is way out of my league. I need to call the captain."

"Do what you have to do. I just want Gracie back."

I called Captain Short, and within a half hour Shorty and two black SUVs were at the curb.

The captain and four men I'd never seen before came to the door.

"Walt, Brother Hank, these are agents Blackburn, Finch, Greeley, and Barnes with the FBI."

"FBI?"

"Walt, kidnapping is a federal offense. The FBI has jurisdiction here. It's their case."

Blackburn was obviously the agent in charge. He herded us into the pastor's study and had Brother Hank retell the story from the beginning.

When he was finished, Blackburn turned to Shorty and me.

"Thanks for your help, gentlemen. We'll take it from here."

He dismissed us with a wave of his hand.

"Hold on a minute," I said.

"I said we'll take it from here. We've handled hundreds of abductions. We'll get Mrs. Johnson back."

"But ... but," stammered Brother Hank. "I want Walt here. He's my friend and I trust him."

Then the captain broke in. "I know you guys have jurisdiction, but it's customary to have a liaison with the department. I want Walt to be our liaison. Just let him know if there's any way we can help."

Blackburn shook his head in disgust. "Okay, okay. Just stay out of our way."

No problem.

The Feds busied themselves setting up recording equipment and computers, and there really wasn't much for me to do, so I retreated into another room and called Lee. I explained what had transpired up to this point.

"Lee, I understand why they would want the tapes, but what are they going to do with them? Everybody knows they exist, and if someone shows up at RCA or Capitol, they'll know immediately that they are the thieves."

"Oh, they're not going to a U.S. company. They're going overseas, someplace like China or Taiwan or Japan. Shoot, anybody can burn a CD."

I knew he was right. I have a program on my computer that lets me download just about any song and another program that will burn the songs to a disc.

Lee continued, "The tapes will have to be digitally remastered, but that technology is available anywhere."

"Yeah, but what about distribution?"

"They're not going to peddle them to Target or Walmart. They'll sell them on the Internet and ship them to guys who'll sell them out of the trunk of their car. This goes on all the time. The unauthorized pirating of new releases is one of the biggest problems in the music industry, and it's almost a victimless crime."

"How so?"

"Think about it. Lady Gaga is set to release a new album, and the pirates get a hold of it, produce it, and ship it to their street network. Do you think some teeny bopper is going to care where the CD came from if they can buy it out of a trunk for eight bucks instead of paying sixteen in a retail store? Who's the victim here? Lady Gaga and the record company, and they're already rich, so who cares?

"There are millions of Elvis fans worldwide, aching to get their hands on the new release. They'll buy them wherever they can find them."

"So if these tapes get away, Brother Hank is left holding an empty bag."

"Yep. I'm afraid so."

"Oh, hey," Lee added, "I hear we're going to perform together at the Sprint Center. Cool! Break a leg."

Why does everyone want to cripple me?

I thanked Lee, signed off, and returned to the room that the agents had commandeered as a control center.

The phone rang, and Blackburn raised his hand for silence and pointed to Brother Hank, who picked up the phone.

"Hello."

"Mr. Johnson, we know the FBI is there, so why don't you put me on speakerphone so we can all chat?"

Brother Hank pushed the button and set the phone where we could all hear.

"Okay, you're on speaker. Is my wife okay?"

"Of course she is. We don't want to hurt her if we don't have to. All we want are the tapes."

Blackburn spoke up. "Before we proceed any further, we have to hear from Mrs. Johnson. Put her on, and then we'll listen to what you have to say."

There was a brief moment of silence, and Gracie's quivering voice came over the speaker.

"Henry, please! Just give them the tapes. I don't want to die."

"All right. Now you know she's alive. Your forty-five seconds are up, so I'll have to sign off for now so you can't trace the call, but I'll be in touch later. You might take this time to retrieve the tapes from wherever you've hidden them. When I call again, things will move quickly."

Then the line went dead.

Blackburn looked at his technician, who shook his head in disgust.

"Not enough time. This guy knows what he's doing."

"What about the tapes?" Brother Hank asked. "Shall I get them?"

"Yes. You and Agent Finch and the old man here can go to the bank. But be careful and don't take any chances."

The three of us retrieved the tapes from the safety deposit box without incident.

As soon as we walked in the door, the phone rang again.

"Here are your instructions. Listen carefully. "Place the tapes in a brown paper bag. Tomorrow, at precisely 10:00 a.m., take it to the intersection of Independence Avenue and Benton Boulevard and wait in the covered bus stop on that corner. A vehicle will pick you up.

"Oh yes, and send it with the old man there."

Apparently they had been observing our activities.

"If your guy is wearing a wire, the lady dies. If your guy is armed, the lady dies. If you follow us on the ground or in the air, the lady dies. Do you understand?"

"Yes, we get it. What then?"

"We'll take the tapes to the location that we're keeping Mrs. Johnson. Not that we don't trust the FBI, but we'll need to listen to the tapes before we finish the exchange.

"If the tapes are good, we will blindfold the lady and the old man and release them in a public place.

If the tape's no good, you'll never see either of them again."

"I'm sorry. That's just not acceptable," Blackburn replied. "We have no guarantee that you will release them."

"No, you don't. But those are our terms. Take it or leave it. Mrs. Johnson means nothing to us."

Brother Hank grabbed Blackburn by the arm. "Just do it. I want my wife back."

"Okay, you've got a deal. We'll be there."

"Remember, no tricks or you'll never see her again."

"All right, men," Blackburn said. "Let's get busy. We've got work to do."

"Are you really going to give them the tapes?" I asked.

Blackburn looked at me with disdain. "We're going to give them a tape but not the tape."

"Okay, I'm a rookie. Please tell me what I'm getting into here. What's with the tape?"

"Do you remember the old *Mission Impossible* TV series?"

Immediately my mind reverted to Peter Graves playing Jim Phelps, the leader of the IMF team. He would get a tape player with a recorded message offering them an assignment. The final words of the tape warned, "This tape will self-destruct in thirty seconds," and it would disappear in a puff of smoke.

"Won't it be a bit obvious when the tape bursts into flame?"

"We're a bit more sophisticated than that now. We'll make an exact duplicate of the tapes that will play perfectly, but they will be coated with a substance that will cause a chemical reaction when the tape passes through the heads and the capstan and render the tape useless. By the time they play it again, you'll be long gone."

Let's hope so.

"What if they get the tapes and won't release us? Is there a backup plan?"

"We'll know your location at all times. As soon as you arrive at your final destination, we'll rush the building."

"But how will you know?"

"We'll plant a micro-transmitter in the lining of your shirt so we can track you remotely."

"Maybe I've just seen this in the movies, but won't they check me with some kind of wand that will detect bugs?"

"I'm sure they will. Our transmitter has a timer that is set to start transmitting thirty minutes after they pick you up. They can't find it if it's not active."

"So what now?"

"Now you go home and get some rest. There's nothing you can do here. Be back here tomorrow at eight o'clock sharp."

As I drove home, I reviewed the plan over and over. I figured the FBI ought to know what they're doing, but there seemed to be a lot of what ifs. I could see at least a half dozen places where things could go wrong. I parked my car, headed straight for the basement and knocked on the door.

"Willie, I need your help."

CHAPTER 15

I arrived at the parsonage at eight o'clock sharp as instructed, and the team was ready for me.

They had duplicated the tapes, applied the chemical, and placed the tapes in the paper bag. They took my shirt, sliced a hole in a seam, and inserted a tiny transmitter.

Blackburn took me aside. "Okay, don't try to be a hero out there. You're just the delivery guy. Do what they tell you, don't argue, and keep your mouth shut. When we storm the building, there could be gunfire. Your job is to get Mrs. Johnson on the ground and protect her as much as possible while we clean up this mess. Any questions?"

I couldn't think of any.

They drove me to the intersection of Independence Avenue and Benton, dropped me off, and drove away.

I arrived about fifteen minutes early and dutifully took my seat in the covered bus stop.

I looked around the busy intersection; people were coming and going in all directions, the start of a typical business day. A kid was selling newspapers on the corner, and a vendor had wheeled his tamale wagon onto the sidewalk.

Then I saw what I was looking for. A hooker in a short black skirt was showing off her wares a half block down, and an old drunk with a bottle in a brown paper bag slouched against an alley wall—Maxine and Willie!

At precisely ten o'clock, a black cargo van pulled up in front of the bus stop, the side door slid open, and a Chinese guy motioned me to get in.

The van pulled away from the curb and headed east on Independence Avenue.

The Chinese guy turned to me. "Okay, strip. Take off everything."

"Say what?"

"I said strip." He pointed a gun at my head. "Then put these on." He threw a pair of gray coveralls in my direction.

I dutifully disrobed and slipped on the coveralls—perfect fit. How did they know?

The driver pulled into a parking lot; the Chinaman took my clothing and deposited it in a dumpster.

The Fibbies would be in for a big surprise when they raided the McDonald's up front.

I had hoped the operation would go without a hitch, but it looked like Murphy's Law had kicked in. "If anything can go wrong, it probably will."

We drove around for what seemed like an hour. I'm sure they were watching for a tail.

When at last they felt satisfied that they weren't being followed, they made a call, and as we approached an old warehouse building in the East Bottoms, an overhead door was raised, and we drove into the gloom of an old grain mill.

We parked alongside an interior loading dock, and the Chinaman ordered me out.

The air was pungent with the smell of sour grain. The place probably hadn't been used for years, and remnants of past harvests sat molding in huge metal storage bins. I glanced into the depths of a bin we passed and saw rats scurrying in the dark.

We climbed a set of stairs to the second level of the mill and moved along a catwalk that looked out over the array of old bins standing like silent soldiers.

A rat sat motionless in the mouth of the chute that filled the bin and watched with beady eyes as we passed.

We were led into a large room. Fifty-five gallon storage drums were stacked floor to ceiling, and a large oak table sat in the middle of the room.

On the table was a reel-to-reel tape player, and a robust Chinaman with a Fu Manchu mustache sat at the table.

Another man stood stoically in the corner, an automatic pistol crooked in his arm.

Gracie sat against the wall. She was not bound and appeared to be okay. I looked at her and winked. She smiled back.

So far, so good.

Mr. Mustache rose as we entered.

"Welcome, Mr. Williams. I trust my men treated you kindly."

I nodded.

"It was wise of your FBI friends not to try to follow. We want this to go smoothly. I trust that you have brought the tapes."

I handed him the brown bag.

"Jin, get Mr. Williams a chair. Make yourself comfortable while we listen to the tapes. If all is well, you'll be on your way in no time."

He gently lifted the tapes from the bag and threaded one onto the deck. He flipped the switch, and the unmistakable voice of the King filled the room.

We sat mesmerized as we listened to the songs that the whole world was anxiously waiting to hear. Louie Armstrong's *Wonderful World* was the last track on the tape.

He reached for the switch, and I thought we were home free, but instead he said, "That's my favorite of them all. If you will indulge me, I would like to hear it again."

I watched in horror as he pushed the rewind button. When he pressed 'play' again, instead of Elvis's melodious voice, a series of squeals and squawks erupted from the speakers.

He backed up the tape even further and pressed 'play' again.

His face turned red as he heard the same gibberish as before.

"Mr. Williams, this is an unfortunate turn of events. It would appear that your colleagues have placed you in an awkward position with this little stunt. My orders are clear. If the exchange is aborted, I am to tie up loose ends and leave the city immediately. I am very sorry."

I figured Gracie and I were the 'loose ends.' Evidently Gracie had figured it out too. The look of horror on her face told the whole story.

In desperation, I looked around the room for something, anything, that could get us out of this mess.

The two goons that had brought me had stepped outside, probably for a smoke.

Mr. Mustache rose from the chair and addressed the guy with the gun.

"Jin, take care of this, please." He pointed in our direction.

There was a stack of fifty-five gallon drums between our executioner and us. If I could bring them down, we might have a chance to make the door.

I launched myself at the barrel on the bottom of the stack and hit it full force with my shoulder. The stack wobbled and swayed and finally tilted. The reaction was way more than I had hoped for. The first stack fell into the second stack, causing a domino effect, and soon rusty barrels were everywhere.

The gunman ducked under the table to avoid the avalanche.

I grabbed Gracie by the hand. "Come on! Let's get out of here!"

We ran through the door and across the catwalk toward the stairs.

The two goons had heard the commotion and were coming up the stairway just as we reached the top.

I quickly pulled Gracie back, and we retraced our steps, but the gunman had recovered and was coming out of the room.

We were caught on the catwalk, high above the floor. A man with an automatic pistol blocked one exit, and two goons were advancing on us from the other direction.

Our options were running out.

Then I saw it.

The grain chute opening into the storage bin.

I remembered the rats I had seen and could only imagine the spiders and other crawly creatures that must inhabit the old bin, but I also remembered the moldy grain covering the floor of the bin.

I hate rats and I really hate spiders, but not as much as I hate getting shot.

I grabbed Gracie by the arms and looked her in the eye.

"Gracie, do you trust me?"

She nodded.

"I mean really trust me?"

She nodded again.

I pointed to the grain chute. "Then let's go."

I boosted her into the black hole and whispered, "When you hit the bottom, roll away."

I shoved her into the chute.

I heard her hit bottom and whimper, but she managed to say, "I'm okay."

I climbed into the chute just as the gunman sprayed a volley in my direction.

No time to think; just leap.

The grain broke my fall, but the impact knocked the breath out of me, and I landed on something hard.

I lay motionless trying to regain my breath, expecting the gunman to fire into the bin at any moment.

Instead, I heard shouting and footsteps, one burst from the automatic pistol, return fire, and then silence.

I heard footsteps coming toward the bin, and a light illuminated our inner sanctum.

"Hey, old man. Whatcha doing in there?" Dooley's smiling face filled the grain bin door.

I crawled to the door and looked out. Vince, Ox, and a half dozen officers from our squad had rounded up and cuffed the Chinamen.

Dooley shined his light around the bin's interior.

"Well, I guess you're going to have some paperwork to fill out. Death by officer, you know." He laughed as he pointed to the huge rat I had landed on.

I helped Gracie out of the bin. She had miraculously come through the ordeal unhurt. I heard her squeal for joy as she ran to the waiting arms of Brother Hank.

Ox came to my side. "You okay, partner?"

"Well, I'm better off than the rat."

"You wouldn't be if it weren't for these guys."

He pulled Willie and Maxine out of the shadows.

"Dat was some idea, Mr. Walt. Dem Chinamen wouda never suspected a ho and a drunk to be tailing 'em."

"As soon as the van pulled into the warehouse, Willie called and gave us your location," Ox said. "I guess we cut it a little close."

"Better late than never."

I held on to Ox and limped out of the warehouse.

Another near-death experience.

But another victory for Lady Justice.

Maybe she just loves Elvis.

CHAPTER 16

My swan dive into the depths of the grain bin, while not lethal, had certainly left its mark. I was covered from head to toe with moldy grain and rat poop. Vince said I smelled funny and made me ride in the back of the black and white.

On the way home, Ox brought me up to date on the misadventures of our friends from the FBI.

Right on schedule, Blackburn's SWAT team had converged on the McDonald's, led by my errant tracking device. They stormed the restaurant, scaring the bejeezus out of the patrons, and left with nothing but McEgg on their faces.

Ox had conveniently forgotten to tell the Feds about Willie and our backup plan. They had their chance and blew it.

I wearily climbed the steps to my apartment. Twice within a week my sixty-six-year-old body had been traumatized by Newton's Law of Gravity.

'Sudden impact' had a whole new meaning for me now.

I turned the key in my door lock and stepped inside anticipating nothing but the empty apartment to which I was accustomed.

To my surprise, the living room was filled with the scent of lavender, and a dozen flickering candles cast dancing shadows on the wall.

I heard soft, soothing music and an even softer voice. "Come here, sweetie. Let Maggie take care of you."

She took me by the hand and was about to give me a big hug and kiss but aborted when she got a whiff of my pungent aroma.

"Let's get you out of that and put you under a hot shower."

I stripped and stood under the steaming water until it ran cold. I dried and dressed, and when I stepped into the kitchen, I was greeted by the unmistakable fragrance of biscuits and gravy and coffee.

I could really get used to this.

We ate and talked, and I shared my adventure with her.

When we finished, she put a bottle of baby oil in the microwave and warmed it then led me to the bedroom.

I lay on the bed, and she massaged my feet. Then she massaged my legs. I rolled over, and she poured the warm oil on my aching back. I rolled over one more time and …

Well, everybody's somebody's baby.

I spent the remainder of the day and evening resting and healing and being pampered by my sweetie.

But as the old saying goes, "There's no rest for the weary."

I had a concert to prepare for.

I spent the morning studying my Elvis concert videos and finally selected my two additional songs.

I had seen the other three contestants. They were young and very good. All three could sing. I was the only lipsyncer left. I probably wouldn't have been except for the sympathy vote and the old-timers who thought a Golden Age Elvis was pretty cool.

I definitely needed something unique to set myself apart from the real performers.

Then the proverbial light bulb went off. It was perfect!

I would be doing something that none of the other performers could possibly do.

I bundled up and headed to the mall.

The night of the concert finally arrived. I was torqued.

One way or the other, this night would be a turning point in my life.

I arrived early and was escorted to my dressing room. I found the waiting excruciating. You're pumped up and ready to go, but all you can do is sit and wait. I rehearsed my set over and over again.

We had drawn straws, and I was last to go on stage. Since the concert was such a momentous occasion, special seating had been arranged for us backstage so we wouldn't miss this historical event.

I peeked around the curtain, and there, in the front row, sat Bernice, Willie, Mary, Maggie, Jerry, Ox, Vince, and the professor.

Celebrity has its advantages.

Tickets were sold out long ago, and scalpers were making out like bandits. People were paying two hundred bucks for black market tickets.

I, on the other hand, had scored premium seating for my friends.

Star power.

The promoters had spared no expense with the production. A laser-light preshow captivated the audience. Then, as the arena lights dimmed, fog began to rise up and cover the stage, creating a surreal, almost mystical, yet serenely peaceful atmosphere.

The calm before the storm.

The crowd grew quiet in anticipation.

Suddenly, the stage erupted in flames as the pyro-technics kicked in, and a platform mounted on hydraulic lifts rose through the fog and flames, carrying Lee and The Krazy Kats. They opened the show with their rocking rendition of *Burning Love.*

During their thirty-minute set, all Elvis, of course, they belted out such classic favorites as *Teddy Bear, It's Now or Never,* and *That's All Right, Mama.*

Cheering fans were on their feet as the final notes of *Don't Be Cruel* faded away and the stage dropped out of sight.

Then it was our turn.

Each contestant was introduced, and I watched in awe as each shared with the crowd their interpretation of the King.

When the third contestant finished, the crowd grew quiet, and the announcer introduced Walter Williams as 'Grandpa Elvis.'

Elvis opened nearly every concert with *Also Sprach Zarathustra,* the theme from *2001: A Space Odyssey.* It was perfect to create a feeling of suspense, and the audience would hold their collective breath in anticipation of his entrance. After watching my videos for the umpteenth time, I figured if it was good enough for Elvis it was good enough for me.

I stood in the wing as it blared through the massive speakers, and at the moment of climax, I burst onto the stage and, as Elvis had done in the *Aloha From Hawaii* concert, opened with *Si Si Rider.*

I wiggled and rocked through *Jailhouse Rock* and *Heartbreak Hotel* and came to my final number, which I hoped would set me apart from the other contestants.

Elvis's fans loved to be near their idol, and he had a segment in all his concerts where he shook hands and smooched with the audience and occasionally bestowed a scarf on an adoring fan.

In my moment of inspiration, I had gone to the mall and purchased four bright red silk scarves to complement the red studs in my jumpsuit. I had worn the scarves around my neck during the first three numbers.

One of Elvis's favorite songs was *Can't Help Falling In Love* from *Blue Hawaii.* He sang this often because it conveyed how he truly felt about his fans. As the strains of this beautiful love song filled the arena, the security guards watched in horror as I grabbed the microphone and hopped off the stage into the audience.

I knelt in front of an elderly woman who had probably been an avid fan when Elvis was alive, and tears ran down her cheeks as I sang just to her and placed a scarf around her neck.

Then I moved on to the people who were most important in my life.

Bernice cried too when I sang to her and gave her a scarf, but Mary just grinned and gave me a big bear hug and swung her scarf in the air over her head.

Finally, I knelt in front of Maggie just as I sang the last beautiful words, *For I Can't Help Falling In Love With You*, and I concluded my performance.

The crowd cheered, but when I didn't move, they grew silent, probably wondering, "What's the old dude doing now?"

I took Maggie's hand, clicked on the previously silent microphone, and 19,000 fans sat in amazement as my words filled the auditorium, "Maggie McBride, will you marry me?"

EPILOGUE

The concert was a huge success, everything the promoters had hoped for. The audience was thrilled when the new Elvis songs, recorded thirty-three years ago in a Kansas City jazz club, were shared with the world.

Thanks to an old black sax player named Spats Johnson, a whole new generation would come to know and love the music of one of the greatest entertainers that ever lived.

What is the force that injects itself into the lives of people, that certainly changes their lives and on occasion changes the course of history?

Why, out of all the dozens of old tapes thrown into boxes over the years, did Brother Hank and Gracie put that particular one on the recorder as they rested?

Some might call it luck, others serendipity, destiny, or divine guidance.

But personally I think Lady Justice just loves her rock 'n' roll.

With the royalties he would receive, Brother Hank planned to expand his ministry to the inner city. The homeless and battered of Kansas City would find new hope.

One of Elvis's favorite songs was *In The Ghetto,* which told the story of the endless circle of poverty and desperation. With the royalties from his music, that circle would be broken for some.

Somewhere, Elvis is smiling.

And who knows what might have happened to the tapes had they fallen into the hands of the kidnappers?

We often speak of heroes: guys in capes with super-powers who burst upon the scene to save the day.

But our heroes were not the powerful FBI with all their technology and gadgets.

Our heroes were a sixty-six-year-old former con man and a lady of the night.

Real heroes are often just ordinary people doing extraordinary things.

As for me, well, I didn't win the contest. A twenty-five-year-old kid from Memphis with real talent won in a landslide.

Go figure.

But I didn't go away empty-handed.

I could still walk upright, and all my body parts were intact.

Plus, RCA bestowed me with a modest reward for recovery of the tapes.

But my greatest gift was not money or my brief flirtation with fame; it was when Maggie grabbed the mike from my hand and made her announcement to 19,000 people.

Maggie had said, "Yes!"

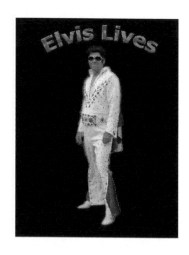

The author as 'The King'

The author at the Kaanapali Beach Hotel
Maui, Hawaii

The Krazy Kats

The author onstage with The Kats

The author in drag as 'Tina'
at a friend's 50th birthday party

The author as 'Herman the Elf'
at an office Christmas Party

ABOUT THE AUTHOR

Award-winning author, Robert Thornhill, began writing at the age of sixty-six and in eight short years has penned twenty-seven novels in the Lady Justice mystery/comedy series, the seven volume Rainbow Road series of chapter books for children, a cookbook and a mini-autobiography.

Lady Justice and the Sting, Lady Justice and Dr. Death, Lady Justice and the Vigilante, Lady Justice and the Candidate, Lady Justice and the Book Club Murders, Lady Justice and the Cruise Ship Murders and *Lady Justice and the Vet* won the Pinnacle Award for the best new mystery novels of Fall 2011, Winter 2012, Summer 2012, Fall 2012, Spring of 2013 and Summer 2014 from the National Association of Book Entrepreneurs.

Many of Walt's adventures in the Lady Justice series are anecdotal and based on Robert's real life.

Although Robert holds a master's in psychology, he has never taken a course in writing and has never learned to type. All 38 of his published books were typed with one finger and a thumb!

His wit and insight come from his varied occupations, including thirty-three years as a real estate broker. He lives with his wife, Peg, in Independence, Missouri.

Visit him on the Web at: http://BooksByBob.com

LADY JUSTICE TAKES A C.R.A.P.
City Retiree Action Patrol
Third Edition

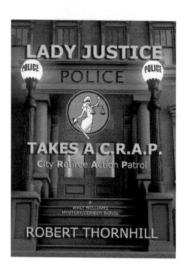

This is where it all began.

See how sixty-five year old Walt Williams became a cop and started the City Retiree Action Patrol.

Meet Maggie, Willie, Mary and the Professor, Walt's sidekicks in all of the Lady Justice novels.

Laugh out loud as Walt and his band of Senior Scrappers capture the Realtor Rapist and take down the Russian Mob.

http://amzn.to/16lfjnY

LADY JUSTICE GETS LEI'D

Second Edition

In *Lady Justice Gets Lei'd*, Walt and Maggie plan a romantic honeymoon on the beautiful Hawaiian Islands, but ancient artifacts discovered in a cave in a dormant volcano and a surprising revelation about Maggie's past, lead our lovers into the hands of Hawaiian zealots.

http://amzn.to/15P6bLg

LADY JUSTICE
AND THE
AVENGING ANGELS

Lady Justice has unwittingly entered a religious war.

Who better to fight for her than Walt Williams?

The Avenging Angels believe that it's their job to rain fire and brimstone on Kansas City, their Sodom and Gomorrah.

In this compelling addition to the Lady Justice series, Robert Thornhill brings back all the characters readers have come to love for more hilarity and higher stakes.

You'll laugh and be on the edge of your seat until the big finish.

Don't miss *Lady Justice and the Avenging Angels!*

http://amzn.to/1xXrYdY

LADY JUSTICE AND THE STING

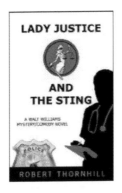

BEST NEW MYSTERY NOVEL ---WINTER 2012

National Association of Book Entrepreneurs

In *Lady Justice and the Sting*, a holistic physician is murdered and Walt becomes entangled in the high-powered world of pharmaceutical giants and corrupt politicians.

Maggie, Ox Willie, Mary and all your favorite characters are back to help Walt bring the criminals to justice in the most unorthodox ways.

A dead-serious mystery with hilarious twists
http://amzn.to/1gS4JMA

LADY JUSTICE AND DR. DEATH

BEST NEW MYSTERY NOVEL --- FALL 2011

National Association of Book Entrepreneurs

In *Lady Justice and Dr. Death*, a series of terminally ill patients are found dead under circumstances that point to a new Dr. Death practicing euthanasia in the Kansas City area.

Walt and his entourage of scrappy seniors are dragged into the 'right-to-die-with-dignity' controversy.

The mystery provides a light-hearted look at this explosive topic and death in general.

You may see end-of-life issues in a whole new light after reading *Lady Justice and Dr. Death*!

http://amzn.to/H20Erx

238

LADY JUSTICE AND THE VIGILANTE

BEST NEW MYSTERY NOVEL – SUMMER 2012

National Association of Book Entrepreneurs

A vigilante is stalking the streets of Kansas City administering his own brand of justice when the justice system fails.

Criminals are being executed right under the noses of the police department.

A new recruit to the City Retiree Action Patrol steps up to help Walt and Ox bring an end to his reign of terror.

But not everyone wants the vigilante stopped. His bold reprisals against the criminal element have inspired the average citizen to take up arms and defend themselves.

As the body count mounts, public opinion is split.

Is it justice or is it murder?

A moral dilemma that will leave you laughing and weeping!

http://amzn.to/1d3FLK6

LADY JUSTICE AND THE WATCHERS

Suzanne Collins wrote *The Hunger Games*, Aldous Huxley wrote *Brave New World* and George Orwell wrote *1984*.

All three novels were about dystopian societies of the future.

In *Lady Justice and the Watchers*, Walt sees the world we live in today through the eyes of a group who call themselves 'The Watchers'.

Oscar Levant said that there's a fine line between genius and insanity.

After reading *Lady Justice and the Watchers*, you may realize as Walt did that there's also a fine line separating the life of freedom that we enjoy today and the totalitarian society envisioned in these classic novels.

Quietly and without fanfare, powerful interests have instituted policies that have eroded our privacy, health and individual freedoms.

Is the dystopian society still a thing of the distant future or is it with us now disguised as a wolf in sheep's clothing?

http://amzn.to/15P5LEE

LADY JUSTICE AND THE CANDIDATE

BEST NEW MYSTERY NOVEL – FALL 2012

National Association of Book Entrepreneurs

Will American politics always be dominated by the two major political parties or are voters longing for an Independent candidate to challenge the establishment?

Everyone thought that the slate of candidates for the presidential election had been set until Benjamin Franklin Foster came on the scene capturing the hearts of American voters with his message of change and reform.

Powerful interests intent on preserving the status quo with their bought-and-paid-for politicians were determined to take Ben Foster out of the race.

The Secret Service comes up with a quirky plan to protect the Candidate and strike a blow for Lady Justice.

Join Walt on the campaign trail for an adventure full of surprises, mystery, intrigue and laughs!

http://amzn.to/19f3XVZ

LADY JUSTICE
AND THE
BOOK CLUB MURDERS

BEST NEW MYSTERY NOVEL – SPRING 2013

National Association of Book Entrepreneurs

Members of the Midtown Book Club are found murdered.

It is just the beginning of a series of deaths that lead Walt and Ox into the twisted world of a serial killer.

In the late 1960's, the Zodiac Killer claimed to have killed 37 people and was never caught --- the perfect crime.

Oscar Roach, dreamed of being the next serial killer to commit the perfect crime.

He left a calling card with each of his victims --- a mystery novel, resting in their blood-soaked hands.

The media dubbed him 'The Librarian'.

Walt and the Kansas City Police are baffled by the cunning of this vicious killer and fear that he has indeed committed the perfect crime. Or did he?

Walt and his wacky senior cohorts prove, once again, that life goes on in spite of the carnage around them.

The perfect blend of murder, mayhem and merriment.

http://amzn.to/1aWGg3K

LADY JUSTICE

AND THE

CRUISE SHIP MURDERS

Best New Mystery Novel – Summer 2013

National Association of Book Entrepreneurs

Ox and Judy are off to Alaska on a honeymoon cruise and invite Walt and Maggie to tag along.

Their peaceful plans are soon shipwrecked by the murder of two fellow passengers.

The murders appear to be linked to a century-old legend involving a cache of gold stolen from a prospector and buried by two thieves.

Their seven-day cruise is spent hunting for the gold and eluding the modern day thieves intent on possessing it at any cost.

Another nail-biting mystery that will have you on the edge of your seat one minute and laughing out loud the next.

http://amzn.to/16VjURw

LADY JUSTICE
AND THE
CLASS REUNION

For most people, a 50th class reunion is a time to party and renew old acquaintances, but Walt Williams isn't an ordinary guy --- he's a cop, and trouble seems to follow him everywhere he goes.

The Mexican drug cartel is recruiting young Latino girls as drug mules and the Kansas City Police have hit a brick wall until Walt is given a lead by an old classmate.

Even then, it takes three unlikely heroes from the Whispering Hills Retirement Village to help Walt and Ox end the cartel's reign of terror.

Join Walt in a class reunion filled with mystery, intrigue, jealousy and a belly-full of laughs
http://amzn.to/17S9YE0

LADY JUSTICE AND THE ASSASSIN

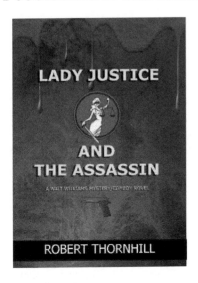

Two radical groups have joined together for a common purpose --- to kill the President of the United States, and they're looking for the perfect person to do the job.

Not a cold-blooded killer or a vicious assassin, but a model citizen, far removed from the watchful eyes of Homeland Security.

When the president comes to Kansas City, the unlikely trio of Walt, Willie and Louie the Lip find themselves knee-deep in the planned assassination.

Join our heroes for another suspenseful mystery and lots of laughs!

http://amzn.to/1bDdrKJ

LADY JUSTICE AND THE LOTTERY

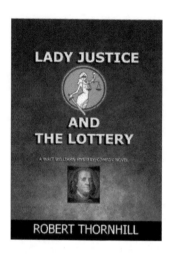

Two septuagenarians win the lottery's biggest prize, dragging Walt and Ox into the most bizarre cases of their career.

The two 'oldies' are determined to use their new found wealth to re-create the past but instead propel Walt into the future where he must use drones and Star Trek phasers to balance the scales of justice.

When an extortion plot turns into kidnapping, Walt must boldly go where no cop has gone before to save himself and the millionaire.

Come along for another hilarious ride with the world's oldest and most lovable cop!

http://amzn.to/1exhji6

LADY JUSTICE AND THE VET

Best New Mystery Novel – Spring 2014

National Association of Book Entrepreneurs

Ben Singleton, a Marine veteran, had returned from a tour of duty in Afghanistan and was having difficulty adjusting to civilian life.

Fate, coincidence, or something else thrust him right into the heart of some of Walt and Ox's most difficult cases.

Our heroes find themselves knee-deep in trouble as they go undercover in a nursing home to smoke out practitioners of Medicaid fraud, meanwhile, Islamic terrorists with ties to the Taliban are plotting to attack one of Kansas City's most cherished institutions.

Join Walt and his band of senior sidekicks on another emotional roller coaster ride that will have you shedding tears of laughter one minute and sorrow the next.

http://amzn.to/17GyE3n

LADY JUSTICE
AND THE
ORGAN TRADERS

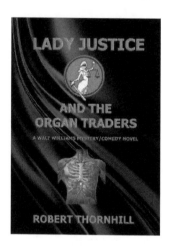

A badly burned body with a fresh incision and a missing kidney leads Walt into the clandestine world of an organ trader ring that has set up shop in Kansas City.

Walt is determined to bring to justice the bootleggers, who purchase body parts from the disadvantaged and sell them to people with means, until a relative from Maggie's past turns up needing a kidney to survive.

Once again, Walt discovers that very little in his world is black and white.

amzn.to/1jmde5S

LADY JUSTICE
AND THE
PHARAOH'S CURSE

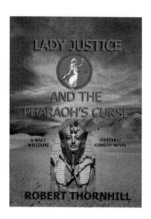

An artifact is stolen from the King Tut exhibit, setting in motion a string of bizarre murders that baffle the Kansas City Police Department.

A local author simultaneously releases his novel, *The Curse of the Pharaohs*, attributing the deaths to an ancient prophesy, 'Death shall come on swift wings to him who disturbs the peace of the King.'

Are the deaths the result of an ancient curse or modern day mayhem?

Follow the clues with Walt and decide for yourself!

http://amzn.to/1yHlnGE

LADY JUSTICE
IN THE EYE OF THE STORM

With the death of a young black man, Walt and Ox are dragged into the eye of a storm as Kansas City erupts in violence and demonstrations.

Fearing for their lives, Captain Short sends them on assignment to Cabo San Lucas where they find themselves in the eye of a very different and even more dangerous storm --- Hurricane Odile.

Surviving these ordeals pushes both men beyond the limits of anything they have experienced, and leaves Walt facing one of the most important decisions of his life.

amzn.to/1w6CthZ

LADY JUSTICE ON THE DARK SIDE

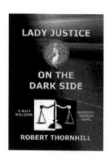

After five years on the police force, a bullet in the kiester from a vengeful gangbanger convinces Walt that it's time to turn in his badge.

Walt realizes once again that retirement just isn't his cup of tea, and with a little urging from his brother-in-law, decides to become a private investigator.

For five years he had served the Lady Justice wearing a white robe and a blindfold and followed the rules, but he soon discovered that the P.I. business was leading him across the line into the dark side and a completely different set of rules.

When Walt comes face to face with the Lady Justice on the dark side, dressed in a tight skirt, fishnet stockings and high heels, he is faced with decisions that will change the course of his life.

amzn.to/1LFIDyS

LADY JUSTICE
AND THE BROKEN HEARTS

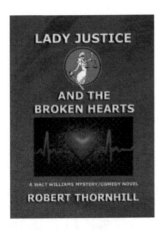

Walt goes under the knife for a heart operation and while in the hospital, stumbles upon a series of mysterious deaths that are certainly not from natural causes.

He solves that mystery only to discover that people on the transplant waiting list are suddenly dying as well.

Then, information about a terrorist plot is found on a heart attack victim who has been rushed to the ICU.

Throughout it all, Walt discovers that there are many ways that a person may die of a broken heart.

http://amzn.to/1I1xTIW

LADY JUSTICE
AND THE CONSPIRACY

Are we being poisoned?

Those fluffy white trails crisscrossing the sky --- some say they are simply water vapor frozen into crystals. Others say they are deadly chemicals, some of which are for military defense, and others to control the weather and the world's food supply.

Are the chemtrails really part of a clandestine government conspiracy? Four people believe so, and claim they have proof, but each of their lives comes to a tragic and mysterious end before they can offer their proof to the world.

Join Private Investigator, Walt Williams, as he searches for the truth and looks for clues to explain the untimely deaths.

http://amzn.to/1Ms5KLR

LADY JUSTICE
AND THE CONSPIRACY TRIAL

Investigative reporter, Jack Carson, has been murdered, but by whom?

Police arrest mob boss Carmine Marchetti, but Walt is convinced that it was the work of government assassins, sent to silence the reporter before he could expose a clandestine program that for decades had been spraying deadly chemicals into the atmosphere for weather control and defense.

Will justice prevail or will the government's dirty little secret remain hidden?

http://amzn.to/23vfry5

LADY JUSTICE
AND THE GHOSTLY TREASURE

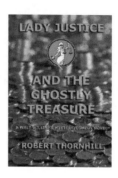

Is there really a spirit world? And if there is, can those disembodied souls communicate with the living?

Can departed love ones speak to family from beyond the grave?

These are questions Walt must ponder when a bizarre series of paranormal events lead his friend, Mary, to a treasure hidden away for seventy years, and a family she never knew existed.

Walt's ultimate answer lies in the words of the Professor, "There are still many things beyond the comprehension of mortal man."

A light-hearted look at things that go 'bump' in the night.

http://amzn.to/235rVO9

LADY JUSTICE
AND THE GHOST WHISPERER

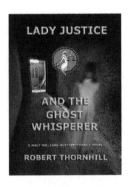

What do a Confederate soldier who died on the field of battle, a woman who was driven from her home by the ravages of the Civil War, and a man who perished in a turn-of-the-century asylum have in common?

They all contact private investigator, Walt Williams.

A bizarre series of events surrounding these paranormal visits culminate in the discovery of a terrorist plot to detonate bombs at a crowded festival.

Once again, Lady Justice pairs Walt with forces from beyond the veil to solve mysteries hidden for decades and bring evil-doers to justice.

amzn.to/2cwzNU6

Lady Justice and the Spy

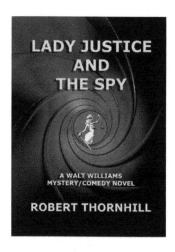

Walt and his senior sidekicks match wits with a killer clown, and an assassin hired by Big Pharma to murder a holistic physician working on a cure for cancer.

Things were going bad when a mysterious government spy appeared to save the day, but this spy had an ulterior motive, and it involved a member of Walt's entourage.

Chemtrails, conspiracies, and clowns are a recipe for disaster, but Walt and Lady Justice prevail.

http://amzn.to/2llIyWc

Lady Justice
And the Cat

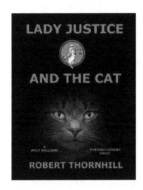

A treasure hunter is murdered and his discovery is stolen.

Members of a terrorist cell who have plans for a devastating attack, recognize Sara Savage, a retired CIA operative, kidnap her, and hold her for ransom.

And who does Lady Justice send to help private investigator Walt Williams save the day?

Clarence the Cat!

Walt forms an uneasy alliance with the feline crime fighter to solve the mysteries and bring the bad guys to justice.

It's a laugh a minute as Walt spars with his new furry partner and the forces of evil.

http://amzn.to/2trBnii

WOLVES IN SHEEP'S CLOTHING

In August of 2011, I completed the fifth novel in the *Lady Justice* mystery/comedy series, *Lady Justice and the Sting*.

As I always do, I sent copies of the completed manuscript to several friends and acquaintances for their feedback and comments before sending the manuscript to the publisher.

Since the plot involved a holistic physician, I sent a copy to Dr. Edward Pearson in Florida.

Dr. Pearson loved the premise of the book and the style of writing, particularly as it related to alternative healthcare, natural products and Walt's transformation into a healthier lifestyle.

In subsequent conversations, Dr. Pearson shared that he had been looking for a book that he could share with his patients, colleagues and peers that would spread his message in a format that would capture their imagination and their hearts.

The Sting was very close to what he had been looking for and he made the suggestion that maybe we could work together to produce just the right book.

As I reflected on this idea, I realized that Walt's skirmishes with pharmaceutical companies, corrupt politicians, doctors, nurses, hospitals, bodily afflictions and a healthier lifestyle were not confined to just *The Sting*, but were scattered throughout all six of the *Lady Justice* mystery/comedy novels.

Using *The Sting* as the basis of the new book, I went through the manuscripts of the other five *Lady Justice* novels and pulled out chapters and vignettes that fleshed out the story of Walt's medical adventures.

Thus, *Wolves In Sheep's Clothing* was born.

Dr. Pearson is currently using *Wolves* in conjunction with his New Medicine Foundation to help spread the word about healthcare alternatives.

New Medicine Foundation
Dr. Edward W. Pearson, MD, ABIHM
http://newmedicinefoundation.com

RAINBOW ROAD
CHAPTER BOOKS FOR CHILDREN
AGES 5 – 10

Super Secrets of Rainbow Road

Super Powers of Rainbow Road

Hawaiian Rainbows

Patriotic Rainbows

Sports Heroes of Rainbow Road

Ghosts and Goblins of Rainbow Road

Christmas Crooks of Rainbow Road

For more information,
Go to http://BooksByBob.com

74727758R00143

Made in the USA
Columbia, SC
16 September 2019